understanding in her own household, but rarely does a fight to change the minds of society ever go smoothly. It's a tale as old as time — as true now as it ever was — and Penland's obvious talent for glorious, sensual imagery helps make the world of ancient Greece feel no more than a single shadow-breadth away."
— Lindz McLeod, author of *Beast* and *Turducken* short stories

Thank you!

A special thank you from the Knight Errant team to our supporters who backed our 2023 list campaign and made this another exciting year in books for our team and writers.

In no particular order we would like to thank our Generous Benefactor backers Argonaut Books, Caith, Frederick Rossero, Barry Norton, Sam Hirst and Charles Page for their support.

We would also like to thank Ian W. and Jamie Graham for their unprecedented generosity and support for the small arts. Thank you all! You, our readers, make these projects possible.

Published by Knight Errant Press CIC
Falkirk, Scotland
www.knighterrantpress.com

Design and typesetting by Nathaniel Kunitsky

ISBN (paperback): 978-1-9996713-8-9
eISBN (ebook): 978-1-916665-01-9

Printed and bound in Great Britain by Clays Ltd, Elcograf
S.p.A.

Knight Errant Press acknowledges support for this title
from a Kickstarter campaign, which was partially funded
by the Creative Scotland Forward Funds programme.

ANDRION

by

Alex Penland

Knight Errant Press

2023

CONTENT WARNING

Blood, mention of death and murder, some references to slavery, manipulation, exile.

For "Niko",

ANDRION

by

Alex Penland

It is the most bitter distress of men, to understand so much and have no power.

– Herodotos 9.16.15; *Calliope*

1

We All Wear Masks

I was five when my father killed the Spartan. When we returned home I washed my dress and put it on again. It dripped a rusty, iron brown. I asked where our masters were, and would they be angry with me for ruining my clothes, because I could not ask my father why he had killed someone he knew I loved. I did not yet know what had happened.

I was five when my father and his revolution took the city of Athens.

I was five when my father killed the Spartan.

I was sixteen when, for all intents and purposes, my father tried to kill me.

▼

It started at the theatre.

I sat beside the boys, draped in the shawl of my himation to disguise myself from prying eyes. The scent of a thousand-person crowd sat upon the air — street food, perfumes, body odour. Athon had purchased honey crackers, and we stole them from his bag to the visible disapproval of the older men around us. Like my father, they preferred the old times: plays in daylight and youths who knew their place in the world.

Times had changed. This was a night-play; new to the festival this year, with all the breaking of convention that the Dionysia allowed. Of course we would be here, us young ones, laughing too loudly and eating irreverently, with our friendships across gender lines and our strange ideas about the rapidly-approaching future. Of course we had no respect. What else were they expecting? Athon complained loudly, Hephaistion and I stole what he'd paid good money for, and together we horrified our elders.

A stagehand pulled the ropes. Now the lantern-owls flashed to life — not the dim, yellow glow of those that patrolled the evening streets, but a blue light, false daylight, a narrow beam created just for the stage. These were round and steady rather than sleek, lifted into the air by their heat and tethered to the towers of the backdrop rather than propelled along a line. Their mirror-eyes shone in an even beam; there was no drifting, easy glow from the lantern bodies.

Illumination. Painted canvas dropped over the proscenium doors: a street, just before dawn. Tri-paneled prisms in the upper levels showed a clear moon and stars, carved into the wood and illuminated by inner flameless light.

The crowd hushed.

This was Aristophanes' latest: a group of women who infiltrated the Assembly, who flipped the gender roles of the city in one glorious night and brought about a dozen absurdities in the process. I did not know this yet — I was about to watch the play, after all — but as the actors took the stage there was a rumbling of laughter. There were a dozen, all dressed as women and dressed as men again — their bright, feminine masks of clay sported great false beards. They spoke falsetto like a second tongue.

Praxagora and her cohort gathered in the lantern-owl's light. She began to instruct the chorus in the art of public speaking.

PRAXAGORA

Stop — if you don't think about your language, then it's pointless to go to the Assembly.

FIRST WOMAN

Give me back the garland! I want to speak again. I think I've got something beautiful. You women who are listening to me —

PRAXAGORA

Women again! You disaster — you're addressing men!

FIRST WOMAN

That's Nikodoros' fault. I caught sight of him, way over there. I mistook him for Kallis, so I thought I was speaking to women.

During my father's revolution, many of the

old orators had been driven from the city, or else slaughtered by our swords, but not the best of the playwrights — certainly not Aristophanes. His work is clever. His words are vulgar. His wit is biting. The last time I'd seen him, he'd winked and told me that his newest was positively written for me. But, perhaps, not for Niko, he'd added — and how could I refuse an invitation like that?

Now I knew why. An uproar of laughter among the audience accompanied my shock of delight. The way the actor spoke, you could almost mistake *Kallis* for *kalos* — my name meant *beauty*. A tease at my father's expense, layered behind a compliment for me. Athon's elbow found my ribs more roughly than was comfortable. Hephaistion leaned over Athon's lap: "Did you know he was going to mention you?"

"He told me to come see," I whispered, still trying for politeness. Onstage, the prisms turned slowly. Their second faces revealed a rising sun. "He didn't tell me why."

FIRST WOMAN

How beautiful, dear Praxagora, how clever! But where did you learn all these beautiful things?

My name again, hidden in the words. How Kallis-like you are, Praxagora. Where did you learn all these Kallis-like things? A sharpness lay beneath the humour. I couldn't place it. It was

4

delightful, of course. It was an honour to be worthy of mention.

PRAXAGORA

When the country-folk were seeking refuge in the city, I lived on the Pnyx with my husband, where I learned to speak from listening to the orators.

FIRST WOMAN

Then it's not astonishing at all that you're so eloquent and clever. Then we shall choose you as our general of women, so you can put your great ideas into execution. If Philodemos belches out insults, what answer will you give him in the Assembly?

Athon elbowed me again, grinning at the mention of his father. *Belch* was a favourite word of Aristophanes, but it was accurate. I'd never seen Philodemos without a case of indigestion.

PRAXAGORA

I'll say that he is drivelling.

FIRST WOMAN

But all the world knows that.

PRAXAGORA

I'll further say he is a raving madman.

FIRST WOMAN

And if the beautiful Nikodoros comes to insult you?

PRAXAGORA

I'll tell him, "Go kiss a dog's arse." And I shall ask him for his daughter's help in writing my next speech.

"Do you really help Niko with his writing?" asked Hephaistion.

"Always," said Athon.

"Never," I lied.

"She helps *you*," said Athon, "and she helps men — why wouldn't she help her father?"

▼

We left the play. I had a boy on each arm and had relaxed my himation to rest along my shoulders, emboldened by my place in the comedic tradition. Athon tried to recall what he could of Praxagora's speeches in a quick, tripping falsetto. I corrected his attempts. It was Hephaistion who was our former actor — Athon had never had a head for lines — but he was busy. Hephaistion kept us from getting distracted in ourselves, kept us moving, guiding us down the street. We wandered like the stars, looping back and forth across the gravel.

The night was warm, lit by pinpoint stars and the low, orange light of the lantern-owls as they drifted on their lines along the Dromos. The smell of lavender wafted through an open gate.

Washing-steam rose from house vents, rising in clouds against the scattered milk of the sky. There was a rush of wind in the dappling trees: cypress, palm, and the ever-present pattering of fallen olives. The crowd chattered even as it dissipated, evaporating into houses and after-parties. There would be other festivities tonight, music and sex and other Dionysian pastimes. Sometimes the boys joined in; tonight, we were all three of us uninterested. We had our own company to keep.

Downhill, uphill, a shortcut through a temple garden. The Acropolis rose and fell above us; the very breath of Athens herself.

I have read the writings of Demokritos, which posit that every item in the world comprises *atoms*: the bricks which build the universe. Atoms, he claims, are the invisible, indivisible, and indestructible particles reclaimed from that which came before us, from that which has decayed. They are so small that their view of the world is quite different from ours; there is the world that we see, full of crowds and wine and friends and theatre, and there is the atomic world, in which each atom sits alone, small and unseen, in the great void that spans the distance between them.

Understand, then, what I mean when I say this.

In our world, under the lantern-owls, with my friends' arms in mine and laughter on my lips, I was truly happy. It was a perfect night, a perfect slice of home. Yet something dark and angry — a twisted lightning of indignation — had lodged in the atoms of my soul.

"You used to come with us," said Athon, and the lightning stirred. "Remember? We'd sneak up to Pnyx Hill and hide behind the walls."

"I remember," I said. "They can't mistake me for a boy anymore, though, can they?"

My father had seen us, of course. Niko had been perfectly aware — and proud — that we hid on the edges of the Assembly. He'd bragged about it to his friends. When I was small he'd playfight with me, sparring with his words, and he'd always been pleased that I could run circles around Athon in any conversation. And now that I was grown, my advice on his work was, in his own words, so golden that Athon should forgo my dowry — with me at his side he'd rule Athens in a fortnight. I asked my father why he had yet to reinstate the position of Tyrant himself, then, but Niko only laughed.

"Oh, for those days again," said Hephaistion. "I hate bringing you reports. I end up defending points I don't even agree with."

"What am I supposed to do, argue at Assembly?" I missed it too. And that was where I paused — could they still mistake me for a boy? How hard would it be? It wasn't as if I didn't hide myself already, when I was out without permission — Niko had friends who'd be appalled at his daughter's unrefined behaviour, and I wanted to maintain my freedom. A little dirt around the jaw, I already kept my hair short...

"She's thinking," said Athon. "Now we've done it."

"Kallis," said Hephaistion, "You can't dress up like a boy and join Assembly. It was a play. It's not real."

"I've been convinced of worse ideas by less. Why not?"

"You said it yourself. You can't be mistaken for a boy anymore."

We passed into the agora. Streets look different in the dark, as if one's stepped into a world inverse. The bustle of the market at day translates into an alien stillness at night. There is an awareness of the absence of life. Darkened workshops. Half-built armour, half-full amphorae, half-alive automata. The last embers of the forges under Hephaestus' temple were finally fading; the death of stars at dawn.

"Not naturally. But I could wear a disguise. I could hide under my shawl, stay on the edges of the crowd."

"Our fathers will recognize you. *Your* father will recognize you. You'd be in so much trouble."

"What are they going to do? Ostracise me?"

"Maybe."

"They can't ostracise a woman. And Niko never minded before."

"When we were *children*," Hephaistion pointed out.

"He used to be proud."

The agora was the centre of the world, at least when the sun was up. We were fortunate in Athens: even in the depths of the war, when want was high and supply was lean, anything from anywhere could be found here. And now! With the revolution had come a growth of industry, and we had technological marvels the likes of which the world had never seen. The automata, the gears, the steam! The *engines*.

Demokritos wrote that the atoms of the soul were defined by their roundness, their ability to *move*. Perhaps once that had been a difficult concept for the mind to visualise, but now when thinking of the soul I always imagine the aeolipile. A round little engine with custom-made fittings, named for the clouds it expels like the breath of Aiolos himself. It spins and hisses in constant motion, the soul of the machine, and here at the market you could purchase however many you pleased.

We wanted for nothing.

"We're not children anymore," said Athon. "Kallis, you can't keep your mouth shut, you'll try to join in. You can't disguise your voice. Maybe *some* women could, but—"

"I'm sure you'll be more than willing to make my arguments for me, provided you can keep up."

"That's ridiculous," said Athon.

"Is it?" asked Hephaistion. "I'd love to see her fight with someone else for once."

"There we are, then," I said. "Give poor Hephaistion a break."

"It'll go terribly," said Hephaistion, ever the source of encouragement, "but you will have a glorious death."

"Fine. *Fine.* You can join us. We meet at—"

"I'm not going to join you," I said. "We're always in three. If a mysterious third man joins you at Assembly, I'll be caught out in a heartbeat. I'll find you there, boys. Tomorrow morning." Thousands of men attended the meetings. It would be less conspicuous for them to be seated next to a stranger than to attend with one.

We drifted north into the Kerameikos, my father's pride and joy. The automatries had brought life to a neighbourhood of clay: new wealth, new work, and a shift in population. Where young men and women had lingered by workshop gates there were now young men and women made of anything but flesh. Serving-girls of wood who poured and mixed your wine; ceramic teaching-warriors, child-sized, with wooden swords and complicated joints; lyre-playing youths of bronze who could pluck simple, three-note tunes. And, beyond, Daidalon's workshop. Home of the true automata, and also of Hephaistion.

This was where he left us — a turn off the Dromos, just before the fountain-house — but first he shared a glance with Athon. I could sense the exchange of opinions in that secret, silent language of theirs: some urgency, some frustration on Hephaistion's part, some reluctance on Athon's, and then Hephaistion was gone with a wave, slipping down an alleyway.

I started for home. I was stopped when Athon took my hand.

"Can we go for a walk?"

We slipped through the gates. Athon nodded our departure to his cousin — a shrill, condescending man who worked as a late-night guard, one who always gave me an irritating wink when we slipped away to talk among the statues — and we left the city behind us. We entered the land of the dead.

I never learned how long this place had been used for burial. Most of the older statues were still, but grand: their dead had mostly fallen to the Spartans or the Persians. Not all. Somewhere there were plague pits, now lost and overgrown with grass and groves — my father had plans to recover and memorialise them, but the project had yet to begin. The markers that did exist were beautiful: life-sized and heartfelt, beloved by those they'd left behind. Grieving faces; faded paint. History, old and stolid and half-forgotten. The old graves.

The new graves were different. Now, with the invention of automata, the statues of the dead had learned to dance.

Where before there had been silence, the cemetery was now a song of quiet, ticking machinery. The discus-throwers spun on rotating platforms. Women wove endlessly on marble looms. Orators gesticulated; businessmen shook hands; horsemasters held fast to rearing steeds. The hollow stonework was beautiful, painted within an inch of life. This was Athens, in all her glory: even in her great industry she was rooted in her past. We lived here, all of us, in a neighbourhood of ghosts.

Athon and I knew where we were going: the grandest of the stelai, and the very first of the new graves. She had not been placed in a position of prominence — my father insisted she would never have wanted the fame — but instead along a small dirt path, away from the busy thoroughfare. His modesty ended there.

My mother's statue could have been mistaken for a living woman in the dim moonlight. Of all the women in the cemetery, she alone was armed: at her side she carried a spear. At the base was an inscription — *beloved for her sacrifice* — and her name: *MIKRION*.

I sat at her feet and met Athon's eyes. "Either

he's convinced you're going to talk me out of this — and I know you know better than to try — or you have something to tell me."

Athon cleared his throat.

"You have something to tell me."

"I have a question," he said, and hesitated.

I waited. Athon knew me well enough: I wouldn't entertain another thought until he asked me. I could outwait a mountain in my patience.

At this time of night my mother's clockwork had worn down: I busied myself with winding the key beneath her stele, then watched her come to life. Like the others, she rotated. Cleverly, she turned on the single point of her spear: her feet moved silently around it, placing no weight on the ground. Her free hand gesticulated to the world, thinking of some silent advice or lecturing some child from a wayward path.

People placed votives at her feet. Flowers. Small pots and jewellery. Perfumes. She was more beloved in death than she had been in life. She was more well-known.

"We've been engaged since childhood," he said eventually, with a nervous glance at my mother's statue. "But... I don't know how to say it kindly. Do you love me, Kallis?"

"Of course. I couldn't imagine being engaged to anyone else." I paused. "Perhaps Hephaistion. I could marry Hephaistion. Any other man would seek to tame me, but you two understand me. You always have."

Athon laughed — short and sharp, nervous — and sat beside me. He couldn't meet my eyes.

"Athon, tell me. It's all right."

"You love us both," he said.

"Yes." I hesitated. "I'm not exactly Antigone. That lust, that devotion — the sort of love that drives women mad? I've never felt that. I've never felt that for anyone at all. I don't think that's *you*, I just don't see the point. Sex is just sex. It's not worth dying for."

That anxious laugh again. He was worried about something, or he'd tell me I was Antigone: headstrong, furious, a lone woman against the tide of a city. He didn't tease me. He said nothing at all.

"I do love you," I said eventually. "I'll do what's expected of me when the time comes. But..."

"But?"

I hesitated. "Are things going to change?"

"What do you mean?"

I watched the pacing of my mother. I wondered who she'd be now if she'd survived. Would Niko have relegated her to the house? Would I have grown up differently, with fewer freedoms? But such a question seemed cruel to ask — I didn't want to assume the worst of my father. I didn't want to assume the worst of Athon.

I lost my nerve. "I mean — I mean that I mean it, when I say I love you both."

"As brothers?"

I didn't know. I didn't answer. "Athon, what is this about?"

"I love him too." Athon's voice was a whisper. "Not as brothers."

"Was that a secret?"

He stared at me.

"You always sneak off in private. When you're drunk, you can't keep your hands off each other. Is this new? Did you just realise this?"

He nodded.

"I see." I leaned my head on his shoulder. "You have my blessing."

Athon exhaled, turned, and hugged me tightly. I buried my face in his shoulder, trying to bury my fears. I failed.

"Do you love me?" I asked.

"Of course."

"As a sister?"

He didn't answer either. He kissed the top of my head. I let myself breathe for a moment, lost in the scent of him and the comfort of his closeness. There were distant noises — a fluttering of birds, a mewling cat, others out for an evening. A youth's voice called — *Dexileos, wait for me, I'm coming* — and somewhere there was music.

Always, always music.

Behind us Mikrion circled in her endless argument, an echo of the past.

▼

My father's lamp was lit. An oddity, but it gave me some light as I came home.

I removed my sandals in the courtyard and walked up the stairs, making no sound with which to be noticed. My fingers trailed through the fronds of potted palms, against the frescoes of our painted walls, as I drifted barefoot to my room. The pebbled floor was cool and slightly damp with humid air; the wooden balcony upstairs was smooth. The house — occupied only by my father and myself — was silent but for the faint turbulence of steam in the house pipes. When I opened the door to my room I put pressure on the noisy hinge, muting the metal, and entered unnoticed.

My room was cluttered. A half-finished peplos hung on my loom, fading with the daily sunlight; worn scrolls were piled in the wooden nooks near my bed. My window looked over the street below, out into the Keramikos. As I opened the curtain, I could see the light from my father's lantern reflected in the ditchwater.

Should I check in? Was he ill? I was the one who wasted wax, reading in secret until dawn's chariot crested the horizon. My father woke early, often before I went to sleep. The oil in his lamps went unchanged for months. Why was he still awake?

Ah.

I returned to my door and opened it again, letting the hinge creak, and closed it with a faint *thunk*. A breath and a heartbeat marked the passage of time.

My father's light went out.

▼

Night sounds.

The running of water, draining down the street from recent rain. The faint song of machinery — a shifting volume as the owls passed in the street, the steady lines of their glow accompanied by lazy clockwork ticking. A distant bridal procession and its overwhelming song. The low rumble of symposia. A lone cart's wheels on the cobblestones, signalling a late return home.

My toes curled against the cool comfort of my sheets and my gaze rested on the painted ceiling. The breath of Athens drifted through my window, slow as seafoam, carrying with it the memory of salt and olives. I felt my chest rise and fall in even lengths, in time with the ebbing tide of night. There are few places as peaceful as one's childhood bedroom on the night of a full moon, or as safe.

And yet the lightning wrenched against my heartbeat. Something was *wrong*.

I had liked the play. I *liked* Aristophanes. He knew what he was doing: humour was best with a bit of truth behind it. And yet.

And *yet*.

Why, exactly, *was it so funny?*

The indignation lurched me upright. The concept itself — women in the Assembly — was a *dream*, not an absurdity. I'd trained as an orator by my father's side since the day he freed the slaves. I was eloquent and brilliant with a wit to rival Odysseus — perhaps a dangerous thought, but a true one. I knew my own capabilities; and yet *Athon* was the one touted as the heir to both our fathers' legacies. Athon, bless him, with his ox-eyes that dulled over halfway through a sentence, Athon who wanted nothing more than to spend his days swimming and climbing trees, white-armed Athon, lovely-haired Athon, Athon whom I adored but was, in an honest world, just *born* to take up the mantle of wife.

He was supposed to be the orator?

He was supposed to sway the hearts and minds of the city?

Athens still murmured: windchimes, shuffling horses, a muted conversation in the dark.

My heart beat with all the desperation of the roaring sea, crashing against the rock cliff of inequity. I was well familiar with the stories of women who dared anger at the unfairness of the world — women who went mad for the sake of men, for the sake of love, for the sake of politics. I felt a cord tighten around my heart, something ancient, tying me back to Helen, to Circe, to Hera herself.

There was no inherent humour in a woman ruler. What about my talents sparked the use of my name as the punchline of a joke? What, exactly, was unexpected about competence or intelligence? Was that so unthinkable? Was that so rare? And why, in every story, was it something that demanded punishment?

I was out of my bed now, pacing the circuit of my room. For a moment it seemed as if I could still see the actors' masks, before me and behind me and surrounding me like a vision, in all the audacity of their colour. I could see the turning of their gears, the tragic faces slowly distorting into smiles, into laughter, into mocking joy, and they were nothing, *nothing* compared to the sight of my own naked face as I caught it in my bedroom mirror.

I had removed the daily pigment: the charcoal around my eyes, the whitening and rouge on my cheeks. My hair was uncombed and mussed from the bed. I was unclothed — no painted peplos, not even a sheet to warm me — and I was a sight wild with emotion. There was a Mainad quality to my posture, a look in my eyes as dark as the wine and the sea.

I thought of my friends, of my father's friends, of Niko himself. Would they recognize this creature in the mirror? Hephaistion might. Athon would tell me to pull myself together; Niko would call me a child. They didn't understand that facet of my cut — the anger, the indignation. They knew me as composed. Competent. And the men of Athens were even worse. They saw me as a girl: precocious and fierce but no threat to their traditions. I was an unmarried curiosity. A source of pride to my father and a point with which to tease him. I was not my own person. To them I had no agency of self.

Which was, to some extent, my own fault. Once you know a person's perception of you, they become easy to navigate. Masks serve a purpose, in theatre and in life.

No more.

If I was to be known to the world, I would be known as myself, with pride and anger and all my sins exposed. Let them stop me.

Let them see.

2

The Assemblywoman

The gods rise above the Pnyx.

Below spreads the polis of Athens: white stone and red-tiled roofs, painted statues and brass automata, cattle and steam and clay. Hissing, spitting aeolicarts rattle through the streets on their leather leashes, weighted with cargo and guided by the swearing tugs of their masters. The agora sprawls in a mass of goods: carpets and gears and aeolipile engines and fruits and wines, tumbling over one another in piles of wealth and abundance, the market stalls inlaid with hawkers and brothels like stone inlaid with gold.

Above is the Acropolis.

All cities have an acropolis, but none like ours: a shining monument to our grey-eyed Athena, lantern of our city, light of our brilliance. Each year we gather — garlanded, singing, dancing — to celebrate the Panathenaia. Athens is wreathed in violet petals and the Dromos comes to life. There are games, plays, festival foods, sacrifices, litanies, contests — and most impressively, the procession.

Priests and priestesses. Temple maidens and basket-bearers. A hundred cattle for sacrifice, and later for the feast. Incense and music: double-flutes, kitharai, lyres. Before the revolution, the ancient ship was dragged on wheels like a simple cart. Today it is driven on a steam-powered pedestal, guided but moving through its own will. Hydraulics make it pitch and sway as if at sea, releasing its steam in ocean-spray bursts, while Athena's new dress — rigged as a sail — billows out in all its glory.

One unfortunate year I was one of the maidens who wove her dress — possibly the dullest occupation of my life, peplos-weaving — but the festival was nearly worth the vapid conversation of a hundred other wealthy girls. When it comes, the garment is hung on the ship and sailed through the city, eventually taken up above the world to be presented to Athena at the Parthenon.

The Acropolis is a place of beautiful things, from the grand statue to the porch of maidens — Athena's ancient temple, where the roof is held up by carved girls of stone rather than columns — to the new and shining gate one must pass through to enter. The Parthenon is the most beautiful of all, the great temple of painted marble with all the gods along its borders. Inside is the treasury: a wealth of offerings in perfume, gold, and drachmae. On festival days, after the sacrifices, we feast and look below as birds sail the wind beneath us.

The Pnyx is suspended between the worlds of

gods and mortals. It is nothing without its men, and yet the men are nothing without the Pnyx: a great stone terrace, the seat of our democracy. It is here that they discuss the laws of our city and debate the future of Athens, where Pericles led the war with Sparta, where my father took power after the rebellion. On the terrace, closer to the gods, they are above the common world of carts and clay.

A century ago, when the democracy was new, we met in the agora. It must have been a sight, all the famous men packed in among the goats. During the war men gathered on the bare hillside, but after the revolution my father had the terrace built. They carved the bema, where the orators speak; installed the wooden seating and the stairs. It's more official, more civilised.

Men favour civility, but I've always had a romantic image of the early days. Powerful men speaking on the slope of the hill, surrounded by the olive trees.

Listen to me. *Powerful men*.

As if I wouldn't speak there, too.

▼

The path to the terrace was long and exposed, a stretch of bare gravel and dirt. I ascended in quick, skipping steps, keeping my face down. There was a terrible conspicuousness to my actions that I wasn't sure how to fix: everyone around me spoke in booming voices, laughing, finding friends with whom to gossip. To hide in the shadows may as well become a spotlight on the stage when one's expected to be social and relaxed. Perhaps I'd made an error. Perhaps I should have come with Hephaistion and Athon.

Someone took my arm.

"Praxagoras!" a familiar voice cried, and after a moment's panic I relaxed. "How *good* to see you, my friend, it's been too long!"

I smiled gratefully at Hephaistion, who was rapidly proving to be a much better actor than I. He'd played women in the Theater of Dionysus before his voice changed. Despite Daidalon's shame and the lowly reputation of actors, I was sure he would return to the stage the instant his apprenticeship allowed the time — Hephaistion's passion had never lay in automata. He loved stories and history. One day, he always said, he would travel Hellas and see where the stories came from.

"You *must* rescue me from Daidalon," he went on, casting off into a conversation-in-progress without requiring a word from me. "I know, I know, I'm fortunate, I'm learning from the master of automata, but he's still, you know, the type of man who names himself after a hero—"

I couldn't resist. I kept my voice low and quiet. "You're named after the god of craftsmen."

"Oh, quiet, you." That had a bit of an edge to it. A clear meaning: don't risk your safety for your wit. "I didn't choose my name, that's the difference. He chose it for me."

I grinned. "If you insist."

We reached the top of the path. Men wheeled and pooled in crowds, passing time before the sacrifice. Somewhere through the bodies the priests were waiting for their cattle; autopneumai pumped air into the cooking fires. Smoke pillared to the blue. I bowed my head again as we made our way. These were not strangers. I knew these men from symposia: to our left Aristophanes was speaking with a group of playwrights, all criticising each other's work; ahead were a group of philosophers who spent my father's parties getting drunk in the courtyard, arguing late into the night.

Niko told me once that the Pnyx could hold six thousand at its brim, and citizens were encouraged to attend every meeting. It was scanter now than when a dramatic topic came to light, I was sure, but the crowd still pressed body-to-body. Hephaistion didn't let me go. He steered me towards the front, away from symposia regulars, where I could see Athon speaking with—

O Athena whose shield is thunder, protect me.

He was speaking with my father.

Nikodoros, whose chosen name means

victory-bringer. Nikodoros Eleutherios, *Nikodoros the Liberator*. Resourceful, bold-hearted, Athens' great social engineer. He who took the mantle of Pericles, who brought freedom to the slaves as Prometheus brought fire to mortals. Commander of a thousand ships. Our modern hero.

Nikodoros, my father, who would carry me to the beach on his shoulders when I was young. Who taught me to swim. My father who called me *andrion*, little man; who boasted my intelligence and wit; who took me with him to the artificer to look at the machines and Piraeus to see the ships and anywhere, really, whenever he was able. My father, who taught me to read on the writings of Herodotos and Sappho. My father, who let me run off to the theatre but stayed up, waiting to be sure I came home safely.

He was my best friend.

He could *not* see me here.

Athon noticed me and immediately distracted him, taking Niko's arm to steer him toward the rest of the ministers; they'd gathered near the dais, eager for splanchna after the ritual. Hephaistion and I backed away.

An augur splashed water — the beast on the dais bowed its head in consent — someone slit its throat. There was a brief consultation before the meat was moved for butchery.

As the smell of the cooking fires spread through the Assembly, we kept to the rear of the crowd. Hephaistion's chatter about his apprenticeship didn't stop for a second. Athon brought us our portions, which was something of a stupid risk. He gave me a wink. Hephaistion purposefully stepped on his foot for being unsubtle; Athon elbowed him and went back to our fathers

As the ritual came to a close, we took our seats on the platform: a high marble terrace, long wooden benches. A great sea of men. I would have been more sure of myself if I hadn't had time to think through my choice to attend; as it was, I found myself trembling. Just slightly, but trembling nonetheless.

Hephaistion rested an elbow on my shoulder. He'd never been protective of me, not like Athon was — Hephaistion knew better. Still, the gesture was affectionate and close, and the moral support made an odd feeling blossom in my chest. Gratitude, perhaps. I was still reeling from the conversation with Athon last night — *do you love me?* — and perhaps my heart was not thinking straight.

My father took the bema now. The orator's stage was unimpressive — a tall dais cut into the natural stone of the hill — but he cut an impressive figure. Strong. Imposing. Dark against the sky. From where I was seated, the Acropolis rose behind him like a crown. His voice struck through the background chatter, although it took a moment for silence to ripple through the crowd.

"Citizens! Quiet down, quiet down. The Assembly is open! Who wishes to speak?"

Traditionally the older men spoke first: today the initial speech was a gripe about the overhead costs of a man's fishing business — something easily quieted by a friend who offered to trade his repair services for a percentage of the fisherman's bounty. He was waved quickly from the stage. I had nothing to say, and so I held my tongue.

Second was a motion to introduce a tax on automatic work, meant to replace the income lost a decade ago from the lending of government slaves to wealthy citizens. This passed overwhelmingly, and with good reason — the coffers of the city had been in flux since the economic overhaul of the rebellion. Taxes were suggested, imposed, and discarded by the season, swinging us between wealth and destitution year-to-year. I had quite a good deal to say about this — once we'd had men appointed as lawmakers rather than leaving such things to common citizens, and I did not understand why we had abandoned that practice — but held my tongue anyway in an impressive show of self-restraint.

Third was a motion by Hephaistion's teacher, Daidalon, to lower the tax on copper coming into the city. Daidalon, who claimed the blood of his namesake ran in his veins. Silver-eyed, forged in Aitnean fire. Master of the first true automaton.

Daidalon was an old and rattling man, greedy, the subject of a thousand mocking stories in our little circle. He had taken in Hephaistion and his sister after the revolution and was, therefore, ostensibly a decent man somewhere beneath the rough exterior, but I disliked him.

"We've been purchasing our copper from Chalcis," he said, "but they know our dependence on their goods and overcharge. So far this cost has been displaced onto the craftsman, and given our importance—"

"Given your importance, you can afford it!" someone called from the Assembly. A ripple of laughter. Daidalon's face twisted in familiar frustration. He was a serious man. He made the same expression whenever Hephaistion dared to tell him a joke.

"Given our importance to the wealth of the city, surely Athens can afford a lower tax on copper! The automatries are already working on margins—"

"Margins!" cried a neighbour in the crowd. "You charged me ten drachmae for a new aeolipile just last week—"

"If you want the latest engines, you must pay for the craftsmanship," said Daidalon. "I could charge less if I weren't paying so much for copper. You know they hardly have a cost at all in Chalcis, they make their money on the backs of their *workers*—"

There was a murmur of agreement in the crowd, but my thoughts caught and lingered on the word. I leaned into Hephaistion, hesitant, and chanced speaking in a low voice. "When he says workers, what does he mean?"

"What do you think he means?"

"Slaves," I whispered.

White-crested waves of discourse crashed from one speaker to another. I alone occupied a space of cold calm. Slaves. They made their money off the backs of *slaves*. I suppose somewhere in the back of my mind I had known that the rest of Hellas still used slave labour — but somehow I hadn't connected that with trade. I couldn't stay silent any longer.

"Ask why we can't purchase from elsewhere."

"What?"

"Why can't we purchase our copper from another source?" I asked, loud enough that Niko heard me from the steps of the stage and looked our way. I turned my face, hiding under my himation.

"Did you have something to say, citizen?"

Hephaistion spoke up before Niko could press me. "Could we purchase our copper from another source? Chalcis is overcharging — could we purchase our goods from elsewhere in Euboea? Or Crete?"

"Somewhere that doesn't use slave labour!" I hissed.

"*Everywhere* uses slave labour," Hephaistion hissed back. "That's not—"

"Does your *friend* have something to say, Hephaistion?"

There was no reason for the hush to feel quite so ominous. The crowd didn't know who I was. And yet — there was no way that I could speak without giving myself away. Hephaistion opened his mouth to try and save me — there were a thousand things he could have claimed, that I was ill, that my voice had given out — but to say anything further would put him under a scrupulous eye that my friend did not further need. I took a risk upon myself instead.

I tried to keep my disguise intact: I kept my voice low and rough, kept my face away from the bema. But my voice is feminine, and it can only disguise itself so much. My father would know it anywhere.

"Chalcis needs our money as much as we need their bronze," I said. "The threat of moving elsewhere would convince them to lower the price. But more than that, how can we call ourselves the paragons of freedom if we still build our empire off the backs of slaves? We may no longer have the League but surely we could convince them that—"

Niko interrupted me. "Are you a citizen, my friend?"

"Excuse me?"

"Are you a citizen of Athens? I have never seen you here before."

"I am Athenian," I said. "I have been Athenian all my life."

"But are you a citizen?"

I hesitated. That was a complicated question. Women were not part of the voting body. We were certainly not citizens in the manner my father implied. The hesitation was all it took.

"Andrion?" my father asked, leaning forward in shock. My nickname caused a ripple of surprise in the crowd. "Kallis, is that *you*?"

The thunder of Zeus himself could not have broken the quiet now. All eyes in the Assembly turned on me. I felt their gaze cut through my shawl, cut through the draping of my chiton, deconstruct me to the basest of my parts. Their thoughts rang in the silence, each man presenting evidence to himself of my true gender: *the cut of her jaw, the curve of her hip, her smooth chin* — and below that, something darker, something more invasive. I wanted to draw my shawl over my chest.

I did not. I dropped the shawl to my shoulders and showed my face. My eyes locked into my father's — the only gaze that searched for familiarity rather than difference. I let my voice ring true.

"Does my identity undermine my point?" Yes. It did. Of course it did. That didn't stop me from evading Hephaistion's hands — he wanted to pull me back into obscurity — and ignoring Athon's panicked stare as I took the bema.

It was as if I had been dropped into the ocean. As part of the crowd one could not comprehend the scale of the audience: now the faces of the Assembly rose up around me, cresting like a wave that would never break. Birds called in the distance. I heard the bleating of a goat, the wind in the cypress trees. I heard my own breath. No other sound.

"It's a valid criticism," I said, stealing a phrase from my father's mouth. "I understand that we cannot stop the other poleis from utilising slaves, but we can put forth incentives—"

"Kallis," said Niko, "go home." My father stepped toward me. I met his posture with my own squared shoulders, my own rooted stance.

"— offer Daidalon's proposed balancing on copper purchased —"

"You cannot be here," he said, advancing, trying to force me to step back. I held my ground. "Go home."

"— from ethical suppliers —"

A half-heard call from the assembly: "— always knew she pulled the strings!"

"Kallis—"

"— so there is an economic reason —"

"We will talk when I get home—"

"Kallis, lord of the house!"

"— for them to pay their workers —"

"*Get off the stage.*"

"Calls her *little man*, what was he expecting?"

"— and if you would listen to me —"

"*You are making a scene—*"

"— *you would know I'm right.*"

We took a shared breath, nose to nose, staring each other down. My inner lightning twisted. Something in my mind was white and hot. I turned to the Assembly.

"*Listen to me.*"

The sound of a bird leaving her branch. A cat's hiss somewhere near the terrace. Someone clearing her throat on a lower street. The look in my father's eyes was, somehow, still unexpected. I loved him too dearly to believe he truly felt the anger and shame I saw there. We were so close — he had to be on my side — and yet the pride I felt he owed me was absent.

Hephaistion stepped forward. "Kallis, come on. You've made your point."

I stepped down.

The Assembly laughed as I walked away.

▼

When I was a child, my father took me to the

automatries. After the revolution they had blossomed in the Keramikos like wildflowers in the rain. I remember the reveal of the aeolipile in the agora: the crowd that gathered to watch the little steam engine spin like a dancer on its clay plate, the possibilities that fired between my father's friends like lightning, the hanging of the lantern owls on their winding lines throughout the city.

Stepping into Daidalon's shop had felt like stepping into the future. Baskets of material parts — engines and switches and piping — covered the walls on over-laden shelves. Hammers and awls and sanding-stones all hung from chains crosshatched on the ceiling; anvils and great casting-boxes of sand, pressed with wax moulds, took up the back of the workshop. It rang with hissing steam and the ping of cooling metal, stank with oil and copper. I did not like it at first. Automatries are overwhelming places, all darkness and noise and heat.

On that first visit, when I was eight years old, the brass armour of the first humanoid automaton was scattered around the room like the aftermath of some mechanical battle. A helmet the size of my torso sat in Daidalon's entryway: carefully cast with images of Hephaistos and coloured with a heat-painted patina.

I lingered in the shadows, playing with Hephaistion, while my father spoke with Daidalon about his work. Time passed in the fluid, smoky way it does for children. My father called me to his side before we left.

"You'll want to see this, andrion," he told me. "Nothing like this has ever been done before. We're going to change the world."

I went to his side, less obedient than curious and trusting, and he put his hand on my back. Before us was a skeleton: a gangling figure of hydraulic limbs and limp joints. It was held up by a chain on its back, hooked to the ceiling like a pig.

"Let's see it, Daidalon."

There is a phenomenon in seafood where, under certain circumstances, a dead creature regains the ability to move. Pour garum over the body of a fresh octopus and the limbs begin to dance: reckless convulsion, not tied to mind or soul. Fishmongers in the agora loved to scare children with the trick — and, I suspected, used it to pretend their merchandise was fresher than it was. I had seen it a dozen times.

The artificer inserted a brass key at the back of the skeleton and began to twist.

I was reminded of the octopus. There was no rhythm to the limbs, no mind behind the movement. The hydraulics jerked and contracted, splayed in a rigid spasm. I had only just met Hephaistion today — I would not show fear — but I gripped my father's skirts a little tighter.

Daidalon laughed and removed the key. He

reached inside the skeleton and changed something — we couldn't see what — and there was a clank, a *thunk*, and suddenly the limbs locked into place. Random motion clicked into simple steps at a walking pace, treading the air. The arms swayed in calculated movement. The body was at ease.

"I've yet to try it with the armour on," said Daidalon, clearly proud of his accomplishment. "But the balance is good. It can walk. I think, given time, I can get it to swing a sword, perhaps even *react* to the world, with the right adjustments."

Fear gave way to curiosity. Every emotion in my heart gives way to curiosity eventually. I stepped forward. "What is it?"

"This is called an automaton," said Daidalon. "A machine which moves itself."

"I *know* what an automaton is." Regular automata — the lantern-owls and steam engines — had been around for nearly a year now. An eternity for a child. "What is *this* one?"

"My crowning glory," said Daidalon. He did not deign to tell me more.

▼

If I were in one of Aristophanes' plays, I would have had a chorus. Praxagora was constantly surrounded by friends, women who could tell her what had happened when she was offstage or announce the arrival of a new character. This was not a play. There was no chorus to ready me for my father's dramatic entrance, no preamble. He saw me in the courtyard and strode toward me, barely bothering to close the gate behind him.

"What the—"

"I have *nothing*—"

"— was that —"

"— to explain, Niko."

Our eyes met again. Stone met stone. One of us had to yield the floor.

"Do we not talk about these affairs enough? Is that it? Are you really so proud? You needed the rest of the Assembly to know you're smart?" He was incapable of staying in one place long enough to loom over me, and so he paced. My own fury rooted me to my seat, as still as the distant head of a storm. "Kallis, I have spoiled you."

"Really? Every Assembly meeting of my life you have come home and told me the proceedings. Every argument you've presented, I have helped you prepare for. Half your proposals started in my words. I have attended in every way but the physical for years."

"Andrion, there is a reason for that."

"I wouldn't call it a valid reason. Women manage the home, men run the world. It's an arbitrary line to draw. I'm not like other women. I'm not meant to run a household."

"You act like it's a privilege to join the Assembly. It's not, andrion, it's a duty—"

"It is a privilege—"

"— and you are lucky enough, I have worked hard enough, that you have no need to work, have no need to face the hardships of the world —"

"I am intimately familiar with the hardships of the world and we both know it."

I cannot read my father's mind, but I know him well enough. The memory surfaced for us both. Red, spilled across my dress. My father's hands on my back and my legs, holding my small self close as we walked home to the city. The ensuing empty spaces.

Niko came through the reverie first. "It doesn't need to be that way *now*."

"What if I want to face those hardships?"

My father changed his tack. A mark of victory. "What in the world interests you about the price of copper?"

"It's not about the price of copper," I said. "You weren't listening."

"I wasn't expecting to see my daughter on the Pnyx."

"Our city still stands on the backs of slaves. Just because we are no longer slaves doesn't mean other poleis aren't exploiting human labour. The people of other cities are still people."

"We cannot tell other poleis how to govern."

"We can use our power to encourage them. Athens built an empire on that exact premise."

"Which was a mistake."

"Was it?"

"Yes." He shot me a look, but it had lost its bite. We'd strayed into comfortable territory. Nothing was resolved, but the familiarity of political discourse dulled the anger. I made space for him on the courtyard bench. He joined me.

"You're back early," I said.

"You're familiar with the practice of closing early in the case of a sign from Zeus?"

"Was there thunder? The sky's clear—"

"We didn't have a sign from Zeus." Niko cracked a smile and elbowed me. "We had a sign from Hera."

"I am not."

"Andrion, you have always been a force of the gods." There was the pride, sneaking in around the edges. My shoulders lost a tightness I hadn't realised I'd been carrying. "No more exerting that force on the Assembly, understand me? I convinced them I would reprimand you private-ly, that no legal action needs to be taken, but I cannot do that twice."

"I understand," I said, and nothing further.

Usually — and unusually — I was allowed to join the symposium.

I was often the only woman present not meant for a man's entertainment, a fact often misunderstood by newcomers and quickly corrected by my father. When Niko did not notice, I would often tease the men into various states of foolishness — once I coerced a Theban visitor into waiting on me for most of the night before Athon noticed and stopped me — but generally I was caught quickly.

Tonight I was not invited. Tonight I was warned off to my room, locked away for interfering in the world of men. I could not focus on reading and so wove idly at my loom, listening to the conversation build in the men's lounge. I could hear the unbearable tweeting of the flutes — not always unbearable but there was a flute-girl downstairs tonight who had garnered favour with one of the philosophers, and it was not for her talent at music — and the rising lilt of impassioned discourse.

Downstairs there would be a feast — small steam-fried fish to be eaten in one bite and garum to dip them in, grapes and figs, eel in a dozen different forms. After, when the symposium had spilled into the house, wine served in fat kraters would circulate on autonomous tripods for the convenience of the guests. In the corners, away from drunken singing and terrible flautistry, orators would exchange whispered deals — *help me and I'll help you*. They were always careful not to be overheard by certain parties, but young women were rarely considered threats. Niko and I had discovered years ago that I could access conversations he would never be privy to.

That was probably going to change.

The loom was not holding my attention either.

I was not supposed to attend the symposium, but this was still my home. Surely I could leave my room to get some air. The balcony was rarely occupied during these events — I could pace along its half-moon circuit and at least see some of the party.

Symposia started in the men's lounge — lazy discussions from the comfort of the klinai, or the scattered stools meant for late arrivals — but guests often spilled into the courtyard, as they had now. The philosophers and playwrights had clustered near the fountain, entertaining a discussion on love. I could hear Aristophanes from here.

"No, no — we must begin with the nature of man and its development! First, there were *three* kinds of human beings —" Ah, I'd heard this one before. Three genders: male, female, and one of a dual nature. We were all of us matched to a pair, with — "four arms and legs to match, and two faces perfectly alike —"

I spotted Athon and Hephaistion. They were engaged in some private moment, their faces serious and close to one another. For a moment I was concerned, until Athon's face broke whatever deadpan joke he was telling and they laughed. I had always known they loved each other. We were inseparable as three until they passed into men's spaces, at which point they were a pair. I had never minded before, but suddenly I was aware of how often I was excluded.

Was that to be the future? When I married Athon, would I be confined to the house as a good wife is meant to be, while they loved each other under the open skies of the world? Would they lose interest when I became a woman, rather than a girl? I had taken our relationships for granted. Until now, it had been unthinkable that they would leave me behind.

They caught sight of me. Both their faces broke into tremendous smiles — relief, perhaps, or just delight to see me.

I waved at Athon from my height and he made a teasing face. Hephaistion, on his arm, put a hand over his heart in dramatic relief. *You're alive!* he mouthed. His talent for stealth was remarkable in its nonexistence. Yes, it was much more secretive to mouth the words than to declaim them to the present company, but a drunken man making faces at a girl on the upper balcony was not covert.

Aristophanes was speaking loud enough to be heard by anyone who dared to listen, telling the story of how Zeus split the double-bodied people into halves, creating the bodies we know today. "Just as they slice apples to make a preserve, or slice eggs with hairs!"

I rolled my eyes — smiling — and wandered back. I knew where this story went. Those who had been male loved men, those who had been female loved women, and those who had been both became somehow adulterers, despite the fact that love of the opposite sex was apparently a cornerstone of democratic society.

I wondered what he would say of me.

I had been honest with Athon last night. The pull that others seemed to feel, that aching for their other half — I had never felt it in my life. I did not sink towards Athon and Hephaistion, not the way they sank towards each other, and yet I could be myself around them in a way that was impossible with anyone else. I did not feel desire — and yet I wanted their company desperately, above all others. If I had been given a choice in my future I would spend it — perhaps not as we had always been, but in an evolution of that relationship.

Together. I would spend it together. Perhaps,

without desire, that meant we had deep and profound friendships, that I had no need for romance. And yet seeing them together sparked... something. I couldn't understand it. I did not want to think about it.

The balcony was wooden, carved and sturdy, and it was accessed by a stair that ran behind the wall. The stair was something of a secret place — the bottom step was hidden by a door, and therefore it was a relatively private part of the house. An upsetting number of secret liaisons happened in the stairwell.

It was also a prime spot for eavesdropping, and in the past it had been the source of many rumours I'd passed to Niko. It occurred to me as I approached it that Niko did not know how much of our gossip had been overheard from this spot. It occurred to me now because I caught Niko in conversation.

"I have things handled. It's fine."

I paused. We had always had an understanding that I would not eavesdrop on my father. Silent communication comprised a good portion of our conversation: we rarely made verbal agreements. Yet here I was.

"She is out of control, my friend."

"I spoke to her when I got home. It won't happen again."

"Today was not the problem and you are well aware of that." That second voice was Daidalon.

I'd recognize the quavering tones of his bigotry anywhere. "She has been out of control for years. Sneaking off with young men—"

"Her betrothed! And she's hardly in any danger from Hephaistion—"

"It's how it looks, Niko." Daidalon sighed. "No matter your beginning, you yourself were born to be noble. A leader. But Kallis — her roots show through. She'll end up a hetaera or worse, at this rate."

I bristled.

I was not a whore, even a respectable one.

"She's engaged to Athon, my friend—"

"And Philo is already wondering if that was a wise match. No man wants to see his son become the puppet of a shrew."

That was new to me. There were constancies in life: the turning of the sun, the rise of the tides, and my engagement to Athon. We'd been paired since our fathers liberated Athens together. An anxious knot twisted in the bones of my chest. Surely that wasn't true.

"Surely that's not true."

"He spoke to me not an hour ago."

"It's no longer his decision. And anyway, he wouldn't renege on our agreement like that." My father sounded tired.

"Wouldn't he? She's already an old bride, and Athon's far too young to marry." Athon was a year older than me. "Her freedom is getting to her head. I'm sure Philo would let you back out. Marry her off now, get her off the streets, and find her a husband she can't talk circles around."

"I don't think such a man exists."

"You know what I mean, my friend."

I knew my father. I knew that the anger which flared in my heart burned just as brightly in his. I knew that he would defend me, tell Daidalon he had crossed a line. I knew he would —

"All right," said Niko. "I'll think about it."

A white fog opened in my chest.

▼

Himation, laid flat.

My inner monologue had stopped. There were no great tirades, no constructed arguments: nothing but vague recollections of my childhood. Niko and I at the beach. He carried me through the waves on his shoulders, taking the brunt of the wash so that I could dip my fingers in the foam. A mountain beneath my feet would not have been surer ground.

Bread. Olives. Cheese. All wrapped in cloth.

The smile on Daidalon's face as he snapped the first automaton into gear. He did not take pleasure in inventing, I thought, but in controlling, in mastering. There was an appeal, wasn't there, in dumb creatures which would do your bidding: it showed itself in the fishmongers and their dancing octopodes, in the automata of Athens, in the rules which were bound to me like a leash around my heart.

Strophion. Chiton. Needle wrapped in thread.

The rules could change whenever the Assembly wished them to. They were not constant, not bound to the sea or the earth or the gods. Law was not the tide. Law was not the moon. Law was not the rising of the sun. Law was something set by human minds, something which remained in human hands.

Scrolls. Fewer than I'd have liked. Just the essentials.

A lantern-owl passed by my window. Heat and light in an Athenian frame, a clay bird propelled lazily on a simple wire. They were beautiful when you saw them up close: blue-glazed ceramic, the translucent canvas of their body painted with feathers. Their wings fluttered in the night air. They were slow and graceful.

Ink. Blank paper. Quill.

The lantern-owl. The skeletal automaton. The dancing octopodes. Dead things gifted life with a price: be useful, bring glory, make a man feel clever. I would not be dipped in salt and made to spasm like a mad creature. I would not be hung like meat and told to dance. I was not a creature

of steam and brass. I would not be set on a line.
   I had nothing left to pack.

3

Echo and Narcissus

Night sounds.

Some philosopher drunkenly wooing a young man in the street. My name. The terrible flautist's crooked notes, scraping on the cobblestones as the music left the house. An alleyway liaison I did not need to further investigate. My name. Some upset horse in a distant stable. A cat chiding her kittens. My name.

"*Kallis!*"

I wiped my eyes before turning. Athon and Hephaistion did not need to see me cry.

Athon's arm was around Hephaistion in what was ostensibly drunken affection, or more realistically a bid to keep himself upright without swaying. Hephaistion was holding up Athon by the waist, his cheek pressed to the side of Athon's chest. The casual affection pricked at something in my heart. Longing, pride, yes — but more than anything a sudden fury.

Did they love me?

Metaphorically, we have always sailed together. Hephaistion is the light which guides our way, I am the fury of the winds which direct us, and Athon is the harbour which welcomes us home. This has always been true. It will always be true.

Unless they chose to change things.

I could see more than the future I feared: here, with the two of them in front of me, I could see the future I wanted more than anything. Long days spent reading, writing, arguing politics. Hephaistion could write and act however he pleased — certainly none of us had any need for respectability — and Athon could manage the house, and nothing would change, not really. We would still have our theatre nights at the Festival; we would have symposia that ran late into the night, surrounded by our friends; I would possess a security of self that I could get from no one else. Home. All of us together. All of us free to be ourselves as we wished.

Light. Wind. Harbour.

Who else could ever understand? Other men were possessive, jealous, controlling — what I had with Athon and Hephaistion would be unthinkable of a married woman. It was nearly unthinkable already. My father had no right to take them from me. To take *this* from me. Fear and loneliness burned in my heart, congealing into a dry and pounding rage.

"Where are you going?"

"What happened?" Hephaistion was more observant than my intended. Athon saw my possessions on my back, but Hephaistion saw the fog and fury in my eyes.

"I'm fine."

"You're not," Hephaistion said.

I met Athon's gaze. He returned the glance with an even, unmoving stare. I wasn't going to vanish unseen or unheard, not as I'd hoped, so I chose to let them in. "Your father is rethinking our engagement. My father is rethinking the arrangement as well and is considering marrying me off to someone who can keep me under control. I am no longer safe here, so I'm leaving."

"But that's wrong." I could see the slow turn of the gears behind Athon's eyes as his inner machine re-oriented. "I can marry you if I choose —"

"And Philo has said before that you need his blessing if you want his estate."

"I'd rather have you than my inheritance!"

Hephaistion interrupted our useless tangent. "Kallis, what are you thinking? Were you planning on sleeping in the streets? A temple? Charming your way into another symposium and *entertaining*?"

"Perhaps I am. Maybe that's the only freedom I can eke out for myself. I'll be a whore."

"Stop. Think, Kallis." Our light in the darkness of the world. I met Hephaistion's eyes, despairing, and his gaze was solid ground. "Daidalon's not leaving the party for a while. Just... come back with us. You can hide in my sister's room until you know what to do. You'll be safe. He won't notice."

My pause betrayed my reservation.

"Don't make that face. Persis can keep you secret. She's practised at hiding women in the house."

"Ah, well, that's fine then. I'll just hide away in your home like all of Persis' lady friends. That's dignified."

"Don't use that tone. I'm helping you. Come on."

▼

Persis was her brother's ghost.

She lived upstairs. She was identical to him in a thousand ways: the same loose curls, the same warm, dark skin, the same brown eyes. But where Hephaistion's femininity was a refreshing point of our friendship, his twin was the embodiment of all my frustrations. I could not fathom the effort she put into her hair, the love she had for weaving. Perhaps most inscrutably, she spent time with other women — she enjoyed the vapid conversation, the unending hobbies. Persis was an indecipherable mirror, a reflection distorted by ripples in the water.

When we intersected it was rarely with words — I often felt as if I was watching a play when she wandered into Daidalon's workshop, asking for money or coming home from some unannounced venture. For all his faults, I felt some sympathy with Daidalon when I saw them argue. He had taken them in, after all.

▼

The house of Daidalon was different from my father's. It was older — Niko had rebuilt our home from the ashes of a house destroyed in the rebellion, whereas Daidalon had lived here as a slave before he claimed the oikos for himself. Our home was modern, connected to the Hydra — named both for the water it carried and the clay pipes that threaded through the city like the monster's tangled necks. We had a cistern in our courtyard and room to exercise around it. We had a steam kitchen and a pebbled mosaic floor.

Daidalon's home was not modern, which struck me with a certain irony. Any and all innovations in the house were experimental: it was littered with malfunctioning or broken machines. Tripods on half-functional, prototypical motors spun in circles along the courtyard with apparent minds of their own, tripping and catching on the dirt floor. Steam vented at odd and random places from mysterious pipes. Half-finished bronze warriors littered the entry like victims of engineered massacre.

They left me there, with my small bag of things and the rage that burned a hollow in my stomach. I laid my himation in the corner of

Persis' room, a makeshift bed. Persis sat on her own bed and watched me.

I wasn't sure what she'd been doing this evening. Clearly *something*, with her hair like that — up in braids above eyes she'd lightened with chalk — but she didn't seem tired. There was an unfamiliar energy humming through the core of her. I couldn't read it. Something brimming with surface tension, a cup ready to flow over. Her brother was gentle and steady, a calm river under moonlight; Persis was the windswept sea on a bright day. Even now, sitting still, her fingers fidgeted with the white linen of her dress. Her eyes darted around the room. Her lips kept twitching into a smile. She was a flicker of motion in the corner of my eye, drawing my gaze despite my desire to avoid conversation.

My scrolls, laid out, one by one along the side of the shawl that would serve as my bed. Herodotos, Euripides, Philolaos. I ran my fingers over the papyrus, checking for folds and stains. They had survived their travel intact.

"You spoke at the Assembly today," said Persis, overflowing.

"That would be why I need somewhere to stay tonight, yes."

"I know that. But *you spoke at the Assembly*."

And look where that got me. There is a story about a nymph who spoke her mind: she was cursed by the gods to say nothing another had not said before her. I had always thought myself Odysseus, but perhaps I was not. Perhaps I was Echo. Perhaps by speaking my mind I had doomed myself to a life of translucence, of living in the shadows.

I didn't reply to Persis. I lay down on the floor and wrapped myself in my shawl, embracing the comfort of my own misery. I heard her sigh as she blew the candle out.

▼

My first experience with Persis had been in the workshop. I knew from Hephaistion that she helped out often, but I'd never seen her there before. We were perhaps nine, on the awkward precipice of understanding adulthood. I was waiting in the doorway to pick up an order of my father's; the twins were casting bronze, and Daidalon was away for some meeting.

Hephaistion was apologetic, bored with his work, but Persis was — to my discomfort — overjoyed at having another girl around. She showed me the wax figures that were put into the moulds to be replaced by bronze in identical replicas. I was reluctant, but it was impossible not to be swept into her enthusiasm eventually. I had little interest in the jewellery and silver-casting that enamoured Persis, but how could one not be impressed? She'd made the necklace she was wearing with her own two hands.

Then Daidalon returned.

Before he noticed me, I was privy to a moment of invisibility. I saw pride in his eyes — the only time I've ever seen the man happy — when Persis ran to greet him. He thought they were alone, and alone, he did not mind the presence of Persis in the workshop.

When he saw me, pride changed to shame like rusting iron, an inevitable and chemical reaction. He grabbed Persis by the wrist and nearly threw her from the workshop in his haste to recover his dignity. When I left, Persis was sitting on the courtyard stairs, crying in small, gulping sobs.

If men have no other sin, they have shame.

▼

I had never been subject to the division of the genders: my father and I occupied the same spaces. There was no sense in his avoiding the women's rooms or my avoiding the men's rooms, since I would have been otherwise unsupervised as a child — and now, as an adult, I was as good as married already. Niko and I were both teased for the arrangement, but it was the world I grew up in. It was normal.

This was not the case in Daidalon's home.

Persis' presence in the workshop was a secret, and men were not to enter the women's rooms under normal circumstances. I would be safe to hide there as long as I was quiet.

The days were dull. I expected to be stuck with Persis, but that was not the case: she worked downstairs more often than I'd realised. Despite the truly strange smells and sounds coming from the workshop below, I was generally alone. Solitude was a blissful reprieve, provided I could keep the Assembly from my mind.

I could not keep the Assembly from my mind. The laughter had followed me from the Pnyx as if corporeal, as if Echo herself had heard it and decided to haunt me. I felt adrift. There was far too much to think about and nothing at all I could do with it.

When Daidalon was out of the house, I sometimes joined Hephaistion and Persis in the workshop. Her presence may have been secret, but it was constant: she was there more often than her brother. She had claimed a part of her brother's drafting table as her own. Both sides were cluttered, but Hephaistion's was full of halfhearted notes and unfinished projects, whereas Persis had small gadgets and bits of jewellery, bottles of ground powders, sketches of new ideas.

I would escape downstairs in hopes of seeing

my friend only to find Persis imitating him at the forge. I had always known Hephaistion escaped in the middle of the day, but I never questioned why the work got done anyway. The first time this happened, I was shocked. The second, I was annoyed with Hephaistion for leaving me alone. By the third, I was annoyed that he had left all the work for her.

"Do you just do all Hephaistion's work for him?"

She shrugged. "Daidalon doesn't care as long as no one sees me and the work gets done."

"But it's not your work."

"I like it better than he does. Half the time I actually kick him out when he's being a pest. Daidalon doesn't even notice." I could see that. Daidalon spent a lot of time absorbed in his machines, and the twins looked similar out of the corner of one's eye. "What did you think happened when Hephaistion was out with you all day?"

I hadn't really thought about it. It's not like my father was a craftsman.

"Besides, I'm the one who inherited Daidalon's genius."

"You're not actually his daughter, you know."

"That's not really your place to decide."

▼

During the day, we had to be careful. It was well known that we appeared in three and so — disguised — I often met with the boys one-on-one. Athon granted me distraction when we escaped our duties to go swimming near Piraeus; Hephaistion provided a listening ear. Persis did kick him out frequently, and so together we'd walk in the country or purchase supplies in the agora.

Once, on the path to Piraeus, he took my arm. I found the question burning in my throat — the one I'd asked Athon — and could not bring myself to ask it. A few days later, at the market, he asked if I was all right with their relationship. Of course I was. Their relationship was not what frightened me.

"Well, something's making you anxious," he said, standing close, concerned, attentive. "I know it's not the Assembly. You're angry about the Assembly, not afraid."

I didn't answer right away. I ran my fingers through the contents of a barrel — glass beads, green and bright — and glanced somewhat desperately at the supplier's stall instead of meeting Hephaistion's eyes. "How often do you think about the future?"

"Not as much as I probably should."

"What a luxury," I said. "I don't have the option. You're going to be an artificer, and Athon's going to be an orator, and I know those aren't your passions but they're bearable to you. Aren't they?"

Hephaistion sighed. "Ah. And you're going to be his wife."

"We both know I want more than that." Now I did meet his eyes, and I was surprised at the intensity at which my gaze was returned.

"My friend — Kallis, it's all right. We tease you, but I hope you know that we're with you. No matter what. You're right. It isn't fair."

"That's not what worries me."

"Then what is?"

"I want more than that," I said again. It came out in a whisper. I closed my eyes to hide — to hide tears, and shame, and perhaps myself — and then suddenly I felt his arms around me. He buried his face in my hair. The sounds of the agora shrunk to meaninglessness.

"We're with you," Hephaistion said. "Do you understand?"

"You deserve the freedom to love each other without—"

"Kallis," he said, almost laughing. "Listen to me. Light. Wind. Harbour. We sail together."

"All right." I tried to obscure the wiping of my eyes. "We sail together."

▼

Night became our liberation. We had a long-standing habit of sitting on each other's rooftops, revelling in the privacy and mild state of rebellion. Now we were limited by my hidden status to the automatry, but Athon visited every night. Hephaistion and I slipped through the window of the women's chambers to join him. There, together, it was easy to forget the Assembly's laughter.

"They're talking about you," Athon told me. I lay beside him on the tiles of the roof. Terracotta. Spotted with the leavings of magpies and city wind. It was still warm from the light of the day. I had a boy on either side, similarly sprawled beneath the stars.

"I saw Bion in the market and he actually agreed with you about the copper," said Hephaistion. "Everyone drowned him out talking about the girl who tried to join the assembly, but he said it."

"How grand." The acridity of my sarcasm could have curdled milk. "It's useless. They won't listen to me."

"What were you expecting?" I hit Athon on the shoulder, but he ignored me. "Kallis, it's not your place. Women run the home. Men run the city."

"Who are you to tell me what my place is?"

"No one! I'm not the one who says it!"

"Oh? Who does?"

"The gods?"

"The male gods!"

Hephaistion cleared his throat. "May I remind you all that we are sitting on a rooftop, and I do not think our good Zeus Maimaktes would appreciate the heresy I know this conversation will lead to."

Athon and I glanced at the skies. The night was clear; the galaxy splashed above us, all spilled-milk constellations. It did not look like lightning weather. Still. We quieted.

"It isn't bad," Athon said after a while. "I would not mind running a household, I think. But I suspect people would notice if we switched places."

Hephaistion agreed, and he leaned his head on my shoulder. "If the world listened to us, perhaps it would be a better place."

"To you and I, maybe," I said. "I don't know about a world that listens to Athon."

He hit me on the shoulder for that, and narrowly avoided falling from the roof.

It is harder to creep back in than out when one is escaping to the roof, and when I stumbled on the floor Persis sat up in her bed.

"Sorry. I was talking to the boys. Go back to sleep."

"I wasn't sleeping," she said. "You were right up there, I could hear you."

I wasn't sure what to say about that.

"Listen," said Persis, "you can't just hide out here forever."

"As soon as I know what to do next, I'll be gone."

"No, I mean — you said they won't listen. I think I can help you with that."

▼

"I've had to learn on my own," she said as we crept downstairs. "Daidalon teaches me more than he realises when he's in a good mood — or when he's correcting me — and I've patched together the rest through Hephaistion or trial and error."

"The rest?"

"The rest of my education." We slipped through the courtyard, heading for the work-shop. Bare feet in the dirt, a full moon, and a clear sky to light our path. We were careful where we stepped, avoiding stray nails and gears. "I can't be an artificer off of talent alone."

"You want to be an artificer? I thought you were fine with weaving."

"Don't insult the textiles. Weaving isn't that different. Doesn't matter if it's thread by thread or gear by gear, you're building something."

The workshop was silent at night. The black forms of incomplete automata lingered behind us, frozen mimics of the memorial statues that lined the Keramikos. Persis found a block to step on and grabbed a crate from a high shelf.

"I'd be the apprentice myself, but Daidalon wouldn't take me on. Doesn't matter what wealth he's got coming in.— he needs someone to cast the gears, so he's fine with me being in here so long as no one sees me. Just won't make it official. But he won't hire a new boy, either. Says he wants to keep it in the family."

I wasn't sure what, exactly, she unpacked from the crates at first. Wood-panelled boxes with odd fittings. Bronze cylinders lined with shallow furrows and wax cylinders with none. Horns. I frowned.

"This is my own invention," said Persis. She started fitting the pieces together in a mystifying format: the horn stuck on with the base flared away from the body like a salpinx, the cylinder clamped into the fittings. "Just watch."

Persis twisted a key. She undid a clasp.

"Sing, O Goddess, the anger of Achilles, son of Peleus, that brought destruction upon the Achaeans," said Persis. Her voice sounded distant and distorted, like she was buried in sand. It didn't come from her lips. It came from the machine.

"O Athena," I whispered, and had I not already been sitting I would have knelt. The prayer slipped out unbidden. "Persis, this is magic."

She shook her head. "You can do it yourself. Anyone can. Here — try humming."

"Humming?"

"Yes. Hum. Just for a second."

I obeyed.

"Change the note. Deeper — and then higher. Do you feel the vibration in your lips? Your tongue?"

"I do."

"Do you feel the change in vibration as you change the pitch?"

"I do."

"The Ionian philosopher Pythagoras—"

"I know who Pythagoras is—"

"— he's said to have discovered the mathematical connection between perfect notes when he heard hammers striking metal at the forges —"

"I don't need the whole history—"

"Just *listen to me*. Vibration is, at its core,

simply an act of motion. Matter disrupting air, which makes sound. These —" Persis lifted up one of the smooth wax cylinders "— when put next to a very delicate needle can translate that disruption back to matter. When I cast them into brass and put them back in the machine, it creates the *same* vibrations. The same sounds."

"Any sounds?"

"Any sounds. You heard my voice."

I picked up one of the copper cylinders. It was hollow, but there was a strong weight to it. I'm not sure what I was expecting: it was sound, so it was supposed to be as light as air. But shouldn't I, of all people, know the weight words could carry?

"I heard they called you a sign from the gods," said Persis. "Let's prove them right."

▼

The agora.

Background conversation like rain. The bleating of goats. A constant underfoot ticking of machinery, punctuated by the occasional rasp of flame or the thud of an arrow from some artificer's demonstration. Worldly accents hawking whatever one could hope to buy. Chickens, chitons, chiming bells. It is swathed like a goddess, draped in rugs and rags of unimaginable colour, dappled with pools of light and heat between the prismatic canopy of shade.

The market is the feeling of cool ceramic on your fingers, the taste of biting into fresh fruit. It moves as slow as oil, milling lazily through the streets and stalls and stoae. It wraps around a person, swaddles you in incense, brings all the world inside its boundaries. Democracy happens on the Pnyx, but this is where her blood flows most vibrantly. It was here that the ancient Assembly met. This is the heart of Athens. This is her core.

It was here that I tried to make them listen.

We were cloaked in plain white. We possessed three clay masks — Hephaistion's doing, custom-made and purchased from one of his friends in the theatre. They bore my face. A large, theatrical version of my face, perhaps, but still my face, carved in clay and clockwork. They expressed large, comical smiles, feminine and kind, but more importantly they disguised my friends. Of course the city would guess at my conspirators, but I wasn't about to put them at more risk than I had to.

My own face was bare. From here I could see the Acropolis, rising above us all. *O Athena Polias, for the sake of your city, let the people listen to me. Let them focus on me. My friends may bear my face but this voice is mine alone.*

We dispersed and I waited, pacing, on the Sacred Way. Behind me and above me loomed the temple of Hephaistos, watching my every move. *O Hephaistos, if you have any daughter it is Persis. Let her machine work.*

I was sure they were in place by now. I'd chosen this spot for the wine barrels — sturdy, sealed, and strong enough to hold my weight. I stepped atop one, alarming the vendor, and spoke. *O gods protect me.*

My voice rang above the chatter.

"There is an illness in Athens."

The people around me paused in surprise. It only lasted a moment — they were a breath away from turning their backs, resuming their conversations. If we hadn't timed this right—

There is an illness in Athens, my voice echoed. *There is an illness in Athens. There is an illness in Athens.*

The agora fell to a hush.

Three machines. Three friends. Three copper cylinders.

"It is an illness of ignorance. An illness of weakness. We have lost our greatest strength."

My friends were silent and still. They wore my echoed visage, just as my distorted voice came from their hands. Following some silent instinct, the crowd ebbed away from my mirrors.

"Ten years ago, my father Nikodoros led the revolution. Our violet city was wreathed in red, but we have risen from the iron and the ash. We declared that no man would ever be beholden to another by right of purchase. Never again."

I saw a relaxation in the crowd. This was familiar territory. My father was reassuring. A few men even nodded along.

"We have been all the wealthier for it. How many of you were doomed to waste away in the mines, in the houses of your masters? How many of you dreamed of something more?"

Something more.

"How many of you were told you were nothing?"

Something more.

"How many of you were told to know your place?"

Something more.

"How many of you think that those words are a sign of times long passed?"

There wasn't an eye in the agora that wasn't fixed on me. A sense of rightness, of home, rose like steam in my chest and propelled me forward. For all my talk of freedom and choice, there was only one path that lay ahead for me. I was Odysseus in sight of Ithaca. Icarus in sight of the sun.

"I have been told every word of that, every day of my life. I have heard this from men who do not know me. I have heard this from other women, who believe the lies they have been fed for centuries. I have been told time and time again that freedom, that choice, belongs to every man. I have been told time and time again that it does not belong to me."

To me, said the machines. *To me, to me.*

"And yet the machine which echoes me was invented by a woman. And yet one day at Assembly showed to me the biases of the gathered men. I think you are afraid, my masters. I think you are afraid that we will treat you the way you have treated us. And would we be so wrong? Think of what you did to the men who came before you. To the men you overturned."

The men who came before you, said the machines.

"I am here today to tell you that it does not have to lead to revolution. We do not want war. Uplift us. Embrace us."

The men who came before me were no longer nodding along.

"Bring us into your fold and the streets of Athens will have no reason to run red."

I remembered the sound of a knife. The blood on my face like water.

"There is an illness in Athens and you, my friends, you are the medicine. Our city has not fallen into disrepair for the inclusion of our metics and our slaves. Our polis is sustained by your invention. We have grown far greater than we could ever have imagined."

I saw my own face in ceramic, repeating

through the crowd. My friends pressed a hidden switch inside their masks and the clay expressions changed.

"Think, my friends, my playwrights, my great philosophers. How much more could we learn? What minds have already been lost?"

The bright, feminine smiles turned along a gear. The clay brows sank closer to the eyes. Comic kindness became an unsettling scowl. I heard the absence of laughter.

"Many of you know me. For those who do not, my name is Kallis Andrion. I will speak until the gods themselves strike me down. I will speak until our city changes. I will speak until you hear me."

Hear me, I echoed. The crowd lay silent.

4

The Theft of the Lock

Before a woman is married, she is meant to sacrifice the comforts of childhood: her dolls, her toys, a lock of hair, whatever made her smile. Marriage is a blessing, a rite of passage, but it's also a point of transition. During the procession, she's between homes — moving from the house where she grew up to the house of her husband. She's between stages of life — between girlhood and womanhood. She's vulnerable. The sacrifice of her childhood treasures initiates that state. The act of sex completes it.

O Artemis Brauronia, you know my sacrifices, but for the sake of the record I shall list them here.

▼

He wants to talk to you.

A message carried by Athon, delivered at the door of Persis' room. It lifted my heart — perhaps he understood, perhaps he'd been swayed by my speech, perhaps he listened — but I've never been easily fooled. More likely he wished to admonish me or pacify me. I'd be told whatever I needed to hear so I'd be a good girl and come home.

I knew that when I went to speak with him.

We met by the Diplyon Gate. My father was waiting for me, leaning on a column of the fountain house. I saw him first: he was nervous, fidgeting with the hem of his himation. His hair looked a little greyer than it had been. A little thinner. His eyes were tired. For a moment he looked older than I'd ever seen him, and I wasn't used to thinking of my father as an old man. He wasn't. He'd been young when I was born, at least for a father: he was only in his forties now.

Then he noticed me. He straightened up. We didn't greet each other. In silence we walked through the gate to the countryside.

"That was an excellent speech," Niko said.

"I know."

Stelae rose above us: dancing women, rearing horses, gesticulating men. The cemetery was not so quiet now, not as families paid tribute and merchants brought their carts along the walled-in road. We took a small stair to the side: into the statuary, away from the noise. For a while we were silent.

"I've been worried about you," Niko said. "Athon told me you were safe, but he wouldn't tell me why you left or where you were."

"I know," I said. "That's what I asked him to do."

I looked up at my mother's grave. We'd walked here on instinct.

"Why won't you talk to me?" Niko asked. "Why won't you listen?"

Niko pinched his nose and sat on the bench opposite her stele. I joined him. Together we watched her silent discourse with the world; together we tried to break this impasse. There was a moment full of silence, tense as the sky before a storm. And indeed, the clouds were heavy and grey. A light rain fell upon our shoulders and neither of us chose to care.

"I'm listening now," he said eventually. "I won't interrupt you."

I do not know how long I spoke for: the rain came and went and came again, starkly cool against the slow-moving sun. I spoke about my frustrations for the future, how furious I was that he even considered marrying me off to a stranger, how much I wanted to have control over my own destiny. I yelled at him. I begged him. I told him I would follow in his footsteps whether he wished it or not.

On the day he killed the Spartan, my father hugged me to his chest and let me cry, let the blood stain both our clothes. When I think of safety in my childhood, that is the moment which comes to mind. My father has always been my sanctuary. I spoke because I trusted him. I spoke because, deep down, I still believed that he would listen.

I should have known better.

Niko was silent throughout my tirade. At

some point I rose and paced, splashing mud in wild abandon; when I finished I sat beside him again. I was an aeolipile on its last reserves of steam, just barely hanging on. When he leaned over and hugged me, practically pulled me into his lap, I nearly wept.

"Andrion," my father whispered, and then I did weep, weeks of frustration and humiliation and fear all overflowing with the single droplet of his name for me. He kissed the top of my head and let me cry. "Andrion, I swear to you, I will not marry you off to a stranger. You understand me? Athon's a grown man. It's his right to marry whomever he wants."

And not mine, I thought, but the words caught on the tears, and I could not say them. My eyes rested on my mother's statue: cold and moving stone.

"Come home. Please come home. I promise we'll hold the wedding soon and you won't have to worry about this any longer. Come home and we can find a solution for this. I promise you, andrion, I promise you that."

"All right," I whispered.

It was the first sacrifice of my transition.

▼

My loom, still gathering dust. My bed, feather-soft. The view of the street. The light from my father's lantern reflected in the ditch-water.

Nothing had changed. Everything had changed. I wore exhaustion like jewellery on my bones. It had not been long since I'd run away but now my room felt too small for me, like I was trying to put on a child's sandal. Sometimes a person grows more in a week than they do in a year.

My bed was Elysium.

I slept like the dead.

▼

Night sounds.

I did not hear the creak of the gate as it admitted visitors. I did not hear the whispered conversations, just as I was unaware of the conversations that had preceded them — the plot that had been discussed without my knowledge. I did not hear the clinking of pottery as the feast was laid on a table. I did not hear the soft footsteps of my father as he entered my room.

I awoke to the tearing of a knife through my hair. My father sat beside me and tied the cut lock with a piece of string, silent as I jolted upright. The world spun around me as I tried to place myself.

"What are you doing?"

He held up the lock of hair in response. Until that moment I had felt relief, or at least catharsis — I was home, and we were talking, so surely I was no longer in danger. Yet Niko never entered my room without permission. He was an early sleeper. He had certainly never been violent.

I touched the fray of my hair where the lock had been cut. Something was wrong.

"You said soon. You meant tonight?"

"I keep my word."

▼

Sacrifice.

Protect the girl, say the prayers to Artemis Brauronia. *Keep her safe*, said my father, even as he lit the pyre. *Bring her happiness*, said his gathered friends.

Herodotos: *Polymnia*, *Urania*, and *Calliope*. Euripides: *Medea*. Aristophanes: *Lysistrata*. Philolaos. Demokritos. Sappho. I had never been one to seek comfort in dolls and shiny things. Each was placed on the altar of the home. It was lit. Flames tasted the flesh of that which always brought me joy. The papyrus wicked flame through my scrolls like a candle, catching odd lights as fire devoured the ink.

Numb with shock, I could not look away. A dull horror spread like frost within my chest.

Protect me? All my life my words had been

my sword. Unlike Athon, I was no warrior. Unlike Hephaistion, I was no actor. Unlike Persis, I was no artificer. I had forever followed my father's path, and here I saw it burn before me. This was not protection. This was not sacrifice. This was injury.

My father placed the lock of my hair in the flame. Smoke, acrid and sharp, dispersed through the courtyard. A wedding, done properly, should take days.

Mine was over in a few hours.

▼

I had not seen my friends among those gathered. By all rights of a girl's wedding day they should have been there, but nothing about this was *normal*. My mother should have sewn my hair into delicate braids. My aunts should have told me the secrets of adulthood in delicate metaphors, punctuated with laughter. My friends should have helped me dress. But my mother was dead. I had no aunts that I knew of. Persis was the closest thing I had to a female friend.

And of the friends I did have, I had not seen either of them.

Niko said he kept his word. But this was not his word. I was not safe. What if he lied? Athon could contest my marriage — and I knew he would — but I would be helpless. If I entered the courtyard and my intended was a stranger, I would have no recourse: either I could follow through, or I could run. I could not fight. I had trained with the boys, but my father's friends were veteran soldiers, and there was no victory in that option.

I bathed alone.

The water was warm, heated by the same furnace that fed the kitchen. I sank down to my nose, breathing in the light perfumes of the bath oils and myrrh. It was a rare thing for me to miss my mother. When I was young her death may as well have been the loss of my heart itself, but a decade later it was hard to remember her face in anything but marble. I had been so small.

It came between long intervals, but when the grief appeared it was just as high and deep as ever. Now it arrived unbidden, overwhelming, swelling in my chest and spilling down my face. I had few memories of her, and those I did have were nothing beyond sensation. The feeling of her hand on my back. A sense of joy in her presence. The echo of comfort as I ran to her skirts and pressed my face into her side.

I was afraid. I craved that comfort more than anything. Her grave could not protect me from the future.

This was supposed to be a ceremony. I would be decorated and blessed with water from the sacred spring at Kallirrhoe — here it had been simply left beside the tub, waiting for me to do the ritual myself. The vase was decorated with a girl surrounded by women, by her friends and family, doted upon on her wedding day.

It was large, up to my knee. Nearly too heavy to pour without spilling, at least by myself.

Would anyone know if I—

Surely I couldn't do that. No one was in this room but me. No one would know if I disposed of the sacred water without blessing myself. Would the marriage still be valid? At the very least the argument could be made if I needed it.

I stood, exposing myself to the cold night air. I dried and dressed in my wedding clothes — beautiful, decorated, dyed in saffron and mauve. I affixed the crown of copper leaves, pinned the golden veil. I tied my wedding belt and draped myself in necklaces, in bracelets. I looked at myself for a moment in the silver mirror on the wall, ignoring the weakness of fear in my knees.

I was beautiful. I knew that already, but I rarely put in the effort to show it. Yet here was the fact before me: wearing clothes worth half as much as my dowry, laden in silver, I barely recognised myself. This was the armour of a woman, for all the armour we were given, with the knife of our beauty on full display. The woman in the mirror could have launched a thousand ships.

I had never felt so naked.

I'd launch the ships of war if I must, but I did not want to do so with the batting of my eyes. For a moment, the steam of the bath seemed to smell of smoke; a touch of incense, of burning scrolls. I shut my eyes against the pain of loss, but in the darkness I remembered. I had not forgotten the words.

Histories. Medea. Lysistrata. Their memory settled in an aegis across my shoulders. Knowledge was my weapon, not my smile. I would carry it forward with me. Whoever I faced outside, I would face him with a blade whet on information. My father could burn all the scrolls he liked, but he could not make me unread them.

I tipped the vase and let the water flow into the drain. My second sacrifice. I whispered a prayer under my breath: *I reject no blessing. Take this as libation. I need your help.*

O Artemis, let Athena guide me too.

And please, goddesses of marriage, let my intended tonight be Athon.

▼

I emerged into a feast.

Symposium is a famine compared to a wedding. Wine, bread, hare, thrush, and perhaps most eminently the wealth of the sea — boar-fish and dog-fish and eel, dancing octopodes, sliced ribbon-fish and bream — all roasted or fried or covered in oil and cheese. Bowls filled with garum and saffron and salt, laid out on tables in oceanic circles.

The feast was already in progress. I stepped into the crowd, scanning the faces, but my father materialised from nowhere and took my arm.

"You look beautiful," he said.

"I know."

"I'm proud of you."

I bit back my initial answer: *For what?* For getting married to a man he had arranged for me, whoever that may be? At a rushed and secretive wedding, full of his friends and apparently none of mine? Likely not for the agora — he hadn't said a word at our meeting, and apparently never would. *Certainly* not for the Assembly.

And how could he know I looked beautiful? He couldn't see me under the veil. I could barely see *him* from under the veil.

"Thank you," I replied instead, and let him seat me at my couch. Alone. There were no other women here.

"I'm sorry," said Niko, lingering. "It shouldn't be like this. You deserve a wedding to rival Helen's."

My heart sank. I forced myself to meet his gaze and found genuine regret there: his brow was creased, and the corners of his eyes were wet. His pupils were fixed on me. Every fibre of my being wanted to forgive him.

"Andrion, I only want to see you happy. I had to do this."

I couldn't. He could be sorry I was hurt and still refuse to take my side. Nothing had changed. He was ridding himself of me, not doing what was right.

"I know," I said. My voice came out quiet, barely audible over the crowd.

Niko knelt to meet my eyes. He took my hand and kissed it. His hands were shaking, just like mine. I squeezed, as though if I held on tightly enough he would lead me into the past and nothing would have to change.

"I love you, andrion."

"I love you too," I whispered. "Niko, tell me..."

In a moment of divine intervention the crowd parted. There was Athon — across the room, draped in white and similarly alone. I had never seen my friend more beautiful. His hair was clean and shining black, his skin golden in the lamplight.

Fear sloughed off my back like a snake shedding her skin. For days the world had been out of sync, a clockwork calendar grinding against misaligned gears — but no longer. The world fell back into place. Athon would be my husband. My father could be trusted. It was an imperfect situation — in an ideal world I would not need the crutch of a man at all — but this was the world. All was wrong, but all was well.

Relief blinded me.

I had not yet noticed what was missing.

▼

In feasting, I could almost imagine the circumstances were normal.

There were songs — dozens of men lauding my beauty, comparing me to fruit and cypress trees, to goddesses. Athon's brothers, drunk on wine with a dash of ego, lined up in front of my new husband and asked for my hand in escalating promises, mimicking Helen's suitors to Tyndareus. One pledged his house and his heart, one pledged all of Athens, one pledged Ithaca — it only got more ridiculous from there. Athon turned them all away in dramatic denial, laughing as he did so.

I found myself relaxing. I danced — there were scandalised howls of laughter, as there were no other women to dance with, and so I danced alone — and I sang, and when the guests began to lift their torches I found myself facing Athon.

There was a moment of awkwardness. We had been unofficially engaged since we were small: the official engagement had coincided with Athon's coming of age. I loved him. I loved him with my entire soul, a love rooted in something far deeper and more intimate than lust.

But it was not the love of murals, not the love of pottery, not the love of ancient tales. I would never be the painted woman who gazed with desire into my husband's eyes, the woman who followed dutifully and without protest. Helen they compared me to, so for a moment Helen I became: the image of some future Paris at my window, beckoning me to follow him across the sea, came into my mind unbidden.

I loved Athon. For a moment I questioned whether or not I loved him *rightly*.

Then he grinned at me. A wave of affection washed away my doubts. Athon was no Menelaus. Any future Paris could not steal me away, for the bounds of our love were not the same as Helen's. Our boundaries were built of gated fences, not impassable walls.

I reached for his hand and took his wrist by accident. I squeezed it, reminding him *we are in this together* — and we found ourselves swept away, into the street, for the procession.

"Not like a brother," I whispered to him, and he laughed, and he kissed my cheek, and I tried not to feel, still, that my father was up to something.

Niko had procured a chariot, painted brightly, and it was into this that I was drawn. The horse began to step, the procession lifted their torches, and the song carried into the night. Athon's home was next door to mine — far too short a journey — and so I was not taken by surprise when the procession turned in the opposite direction.

▼

Before the revolution.

My mother was alive. We were slaves still, although I did not fully understand the meaning of it. I knew that I had work and chores to do. I knew that I could not truly befriend the master's children, though none of us fully understood why. I was willful and impudent, though surely with time they would have beaten it from me.

I was five.

The Spartan had been staying on the estate for some time. My parents made it clear: I was to tell no one, to actively deny his existence, unless they told me otherwise. Our duties to the masters of the house were liminal, often bringing us from Athens to the countryside and back, and so it was our responsibility to keep him fed with fish and information alike.

On those days, my father would carry me with him into the chora, the farmland. I played in the low-lying branches or held baskets as he beat the olive trees. I ran through the groves in wild hunts, telling stories to myself: I was Atalanta, though I would never fall for golden apples. I was Odysseus, though I would never be so foolish as to tell my enemy my name.

The Spartan was bored, just like me. Our masters did not know he was living in the farmhouse. In their place, who would have noticed? When they visited, there were so many of us — surely they would not see a single extra man. They did not notice when my parents lingered in the chora at the end of a long day. They did not notice the plot as it was woven in the olive grove.

Where I was easily distracted from my work, he had no work to speak of — not when my parents were busy — and so he took it upon himself to teach me. He told me stories of powerful Lakonian women, women who trained to fight in childhood. He taught me how to throw a punch without hurting my thumb, how to break a man's grip on my wrist. He told me that I would always have the element of surprise on my side: no one expected a little girl to fight back.

He taught me to write.

The Spartan shaped my fingers around a sprig of olive and showed me how to measure out and mark the circle of theta, the lines of eta, sigma's curling lock. The day my father killed him, I was writing letters in the dust.

I had been glad when my father walked me to the chora that morning. I had thought nothing of the way he set me in the Spartan's arms. That evening, when I saw my father returning among the long shadows of sunset, along the path striped black by the olive grove, I did not even think to run to him.

I don't remember feeling unsafe. The chora and the farmhouse had always been less dangerous than the city. When my father came to fetch me, I was accustomed to being swept into his arms, kissed, called andrion even then.

I was not accustomed to his stopping some distance away instead. I was not prepared for his chiton to be smeared with copper-brown — my child eyes saw mud — or for his voice to sound so low, so broken.

"It's done."

The Spartan was the one who picked me up, who balanced me on his hip like a mother. He smiled, played with my hair. His beard was short and dark. His eyes, as I remember them, were kind. The men spoke, but I was so young — I don't remember what they said. I did not notice their voices rise in intensity, nor did I understand that they were arguing. They talked long enough to bore me, for me to squirm in a request for freedom, for the Spartan's hold to tighten to pain on my arm.

He was right: no man expected a little girl to fight back. I twisted. He dropped me.

My father lunged forward.

I don't know what I'd expected death to sound

like. I hadn't expected it to make the sound of a knife cutting into fresh lamb. I hadn't expected to hear it in the roar of my father's voice. The Spartan's blood coloured me; my face and body were wet with it. My dress was not copper like my father's, but fresh and red.

I loved the Spartan, the way that children do, but I do not remember crying. I do not remember hurt. In all truth, I hardly remember anything. The days after the revolution are mottled and white: blank parchment. There is simply before, when the people I loved were mostly alive, and after, when my family comprised only my father and myself.

What others have told me has filled in what I do not remember: that the Spartan had threatened to steal me away as ransom, and that my father slew him in return for his ingratitude. I had always believed the story. It was Niko's story. And yet…

My father had hoped to spare me the sight of violence. He intended to protect me. To keep me safe. As he has so often said, he wanted to keep me innocent of the hardships in the world, to keep me fair and free of burden. He meant well. I know he meant well.

It didn't matter in the end.

He failed.

▼

We marched up the Sacred Way, bellowing our wedding songs. We passed through the Diplyon Gate, passing the great marble walls, the Talos Hoplites automata which stood in eternal guard around our city. We passed the dancing graves, the gesticulating facades and spinning statues.

We entered the chora. Gravel road gave way to dirt; homes gave way to farmland. Night gave way to dawn, and the black stripes of the olive groves stretched across our path. As we left Athens behind, so too we left the pretence of a wedding. The song died down. The torches, once lifted high, were brought comfortably to shoulder height. Chatter turned to silence.

I looked to Athon in confusion, but he was just as lost as me. I looked to Hephaistion for clarification, and suddenly realised that he was not there.

My stomach went cold.

The procession came to a stop at the side of the road. I stepped off the chariot. Someone, at some point, had handed Athon an apple — as a husband is meant to give his wife before they enter the bridal chamber. She takes her first sustenance from him as a symbol of all he will provide thereafter, and the wedding party showers them with violets and other favours as they slip away.

Ideally, she'll have arrived at her new home. Not some nowhere in the chora, not if you're meant to live in Athens. Not a campsite. Not a leaning, hastily-pitched tent. My father spoke.

"Citizens," he said, in a voice as clear as thunder, "the Assembly is open. We have one order of business. Do we wish to hold an ostracism this year?"

Yes, came the echo around us. The men spoke as one.

The Assembly was not required to meet on the Pnyx. Once they had met in the agora; now, if they chose, they could meet in the countryside. The power of Athens lay with its people, not its place.

I took Athon's wrist again, as if possessing him would help me keep him safe. It would not. We were sailing blind. "You can't do this. Athon hasn't done anything wrong. We haven't held an ostracism since—"

"Citizens of the Assembly," said Niko, interrupting me, ignoring me, refusing to meet my eyes, "are we ready now to cast our votes?"

Yes, said the echo.

"This isn't how it works," I said. "We need time to make our case. This should take months to plan. We have to defend ourselves."

"Citizens of the Assembly," said Niko, "cast your votes."

Ostraka were produced. The small ceramic tablets — fragments of broken pottery, or coin-sized fired clay — all bore one name. An assemblyman I did not know gathered the ostraka into a cup. He read the name aloud — the same name, over and over. It wasn't mine. Women cannot be ostracised.

ATHON. Scratched in sprawling letters.

"Athon—" my father began, before pausing to restart with his full name. "Athanasios of Athens, you are banished from our city for ten full years."

"You can't do this to us," I whispered.

"When you return so will be your land returned, your home, and the dowry of your bride."

"He didn't do anything! We didn't even pack!"

"Effective immediately, you are not allowed within the city walls."

My uselessness rang hollow in my chest.

"It's done, Kallis."

The assemblyman took the votes and upended the cup, showering us with clay instead of violets. Not another word was spoken by the men.

They left us there.

▼

Dawn crested the horizon as she always did, with the audacity to ignore that the world had changed. I'd paced and raged at their retreating backs, but my fury is not worth reporting: it had no effect, and it does not show me at my best. Athon could not take his eyes off the road to Athens. I could not bear to look at it at all. The image of Hephaistion appearing through the dust was intense, a searing twist of need and fear. I wanted to find him and beg him to join us. I wanted to abandon him, to cast him off my sinking ship.

I wanted to scream. I had screamed. Now my throat was sore.

Eventually I sat beside Athon in the dirt. Wordlessly, he handed me the apple. Atalanta and Melanion. Persephone and Hades. This was not the story I wanted, but it was the story I was given. I took it without ceremony. We were wedded.

"Kallis?"

"Yeah?"

"What now?"

The music of the day began to rise around us. A breath of wind through the trees. Workers chatting in the distance. Birds. Insects. The silence of the countryside like a cushion under sound.

A girl is supposed to sacrifice her childhood. Not her life. Not her city. Not her future. *Bring us into your fold and the streets of Athens will have no reason to run red.* I had made my terms clear. This was more than an act of aggression: this was an act of war. *No one expects a little girl to fight back.*

"We're going to Thebes," I said. The foundations of a plan were already beginning to coalesce. My future spread before me: no longer a destiny but a map, full of sprawling, branching paths. "Just until we can get word to Persis and Hephaistion. Then Corinth. And Sparta. We'll gather all of Hellas if we have to."

"Why?"

"Niko won't listen to reason. We have no other choice." I looked at the sky. It was blue and shining, with no storm on the horizon. Nevertheless, the wind was rising. I bit into the apple. "You know, he's always compared me to Odysseus? Too proud and clever for my own good? Always lost on a road of my own design?"

Usually he'd make some joke about that. *We know, Kallis. You're proud of it.* Not today. Athon just shivered.

"He's fucking wrong. We're not doing that story. Understand? We're not going to wander until the gods let us return. We will not allow some greater power to separate us from our family. We've been wronged. We've been insulted. I'm not Odysseus, I'm Agamemnon. We're not losing Hephaistion. And I'm taking my city back."

ΤΕΛΟΣ

NOTE ON TRANSLATION

All translations are my own. I would like to add special thanks to the Perseus Digital Library (an invaluable resource), Dr. Joshua Langseth (who was both my initial Greek teacher and my language checker for the dissertation draft), and Anthi Chemariou (who has answered many ridiculous questions about Modern Greek over the course of our friendship).

GLOSSARY

A

Aristophanes – a comic playwright (446-386 BCE). He was known to his contemporaries as the most convincing author of Athenian daily life. While his works were not as feminist as they appear here (Kallis has some valid criticisms), his works were highly influential and anti-war.

Agora – a marketplace. The Athenian agora was famous for its abundance, even in the middle of the Peloponnesian War. The route that Kallis and the boys take back from the play is still accessible in part today through the Athenian archaeological site; it did not, however, hold automata at any time.

Amphorae – large oblong pots. Mainly used for the transport and storage of goods such as wine or olive oil, but highly-decorated amphorae were also presented as prizes.

Antikythera Mechanism – not actually mentioned in-text, but as it was a major source of inspiration for the story I've included it here. The Antikythera Mechanism is an ancient analogue computer, dating from somewhere between 200 and 80 BCE. It consists of 37 bronze gears and is capable of predicting eclipses, calculating a year, and calculating the timing of various panhellenic games. It is currently displayed in the National Archaeological Museum in Athens.

Aeolipile – an ancient steam engine. In the real world, this was invented by Hero of Alexandra in the first century CE; Daidalon here has invented it a few centuries earlier. The aeolipile of the book is smaller and more compact than Hero's version, but still works off the same principles.

Aiolos – a god of the winds in Greek mythology.

Automaton/automatry – automaton is a word in ancient Greek which means 'acting of one's own will'. Automatons have existed in legend since the 16th century BCE in the form of moving statues or automatic doors (both of which were technologies available in the ancient world, but often guarded secretly and attributed to the gods). Pindar, fictionally a contemporary of Kallis, suggested in real history that the island of Rhodes had moving statues similar to the dancing graves in the book, and wooden serving girls who could walk and pour wine were real mechanical curiosities. Automatry is a word invented for the story, which is simply a workshop where automatons were regularly made.

Autopneuma – from *autos*, self, and *pneuma*, breath. A small automated bellows to keep a fire alive.

Aegis – a device of protection. May have originally held the connotation of being shielded from your enemies by the powers of Zeus (e.g. a thunderstorm) but is more commonly accepted to be some sort of shield of a deity, such as Athena's shield with a gorgon's head.

Augur – a priest who reads the signs of the gods in the entrails of a sacrifice.

B

Bema – the podium upon which orators spoke to the Athenian Assembly. It still stands in Athens, though the rest of the construction is gone.

C

Chorus – a group of characters who comment upon the action of a play.

Chiton – an object of clothing which fastens at the shoulders. Worn by men and women alike.

Chora – the countryside around a city-state.

D

Dionysia – festival of Dionysos.

Dromos – main street of Athens.

Drachma – currency of Ancient Greece. Each city-state had its own form of currency, but the Athenian 'owl' coin was widely accepted.

G

Galaxias – Ancient Greek for the Milky Way, derived from the word for 'milk'. Greek mythology states that the white band of stars across the sky was formed when Hera ripped the hungry infant Herakles from her breast, spilling milk across the sky.

Garum – a Roman condiment made of fermented fish. I've used it here because I found mentions of 'fish sauce' in not only ancient recipes but also several of Aristophanes' plays, but could not find the actual name of the sauce. Garum was likely quite similar and as close a term as I could get. Additionally, the dancing octopodes are not based in historical fact but in science: soy sauce, when poured on fresh squid, has this effect. The sodium in the sauce causes the synapses to fire, causing the animal to look somewhat 'alive'. Garum, which was also sodium-rich, would theoretically have the same outcome.

H

Himation – a shawl.

Hellas – 'Greece', sort of. The idea of Greece as a nation did not exist in Classical times. Rather, Hellas was viewed as a collection of city-states who shared the same gods and similar traditions. In modern usage, Elláda refers to Greece (though Hellas is often used by foreigners as well).

Hetaera – a courtesan. Successful hetaerae were often highly independent women; this was one of the few jobs a woman could do and (mostly) keep her freedom, at least in Athens.

K
Kithara – a seven-stringed lyre.
Kline – a reclining couch.

M
Mainad – a follower of Dionysos. More commonly known in the Anglosphere as the 'Bacchae', these were followers of the god who intoxicated themselves into a dancing, dangerous frenzy. They were known for tearing bodies (both human and animal) apart with their bare hands.

Metic – a non-citizen resident of Athens.

O
Oikos – a household. It refers both to the physical house and the matters of the family which dwell there.

P
Pnyx – the hill upon which the Athenian Assembly met.

Peplos – a feminine article of clothing, similar to a long dress.

Polis – a city-state.

Panathenaia – a major Athenian festival, in

which a new peplos was presented to the statue of Athena on the Acropolis.

S

Stela – a large stone slab, often engraved (or mechanised, in the novella) for use as a funerary marker.

Strophion – also called a strophic, this was the bra of the Classical period.

Symposium – I have used the Latin spelling here due to its overwhelming familiarity as a term in English. The word is symposion in Greek; an after-dinner drinking party which served as a vehicle for educated men to debate politics, philosophy, and science. Women in attendance were generally entertainers — flute-players or hetaerae. The respectable daughter of an orator would never be in attendance; when Kallis attends, she is breaking gender norms.

Splanchna – the viscera of a sacrifice, which were roasted on a fire and distributed to the most important citizens in attendance.

Stoa – a long, covered porch lined by columns in ancient architecture. There is a reconstruction of a stoa in the Athenian Agora archaeological site.

ACKNOWLEDGEMENTS

If you don't want to read the rest, I'll summarize this first: I'm going to thank the community who helped in making this book happen. I'll be doing this in no particular order of gratitude, but this is my first book with only my name on it, so it's going to be long. (I will, however, thank you to read it all, as it is quite important to me and also you are in it.)

First, of course, I would love to thank my publisher. Nathaniel — and Knight Errant Press — thank you for taking this weird little book on. Thank you for keeping this weird little book when I went to Greece for five weeks, told you to hold off on editing, and sent you a substantially changed draft after you'd already accepted the book for publication. That took a lot of trust. I think I've made it worth it.

Second, thank you to the Creative Writing team at the University of Edinburgh for giving me a space in which to pursue this story. *Andrion* began as a failed NaNoWriMo project in 2016: it first fell to the wayside because of the notable election of that year, regained steam later in the month for the same reason, and then was placed aside semi-permanently once I realised I did not have access to the resources I needed to do it justice. When I came to the University of Edinburgh in 2019, I was finally able to tackle the story. Miriam Gamble, my MSc dissertation supervisor, deserves special mention here — hers were the first set of eyes to see the words. I'd also love to thank everyone in my master's cohort who read bits and pieces or were otherwise present on this endeavor. (I'm a bit afraid to mention you all by name for fear of missing someone vital, but you know who you are and I am forever grateful. But also, Workshop Four, Bhavs and Anthi, and the Phrogs, take a special shout-out). I'm also grateful to the Classics researchers who read and advised me on the historical aspects of this story. Dr. David Lewis, thank you for letting me sit in on your economics class and introducing me to Aristophanes. Dr. Joshua Langseth, from the moment I sat down to take Ancient Greek 101, thank you for being my mentor in Classical Studies — your insight on the dissertation draft of this novella has inspired some of my favorite scenes. And, finally, of course, I would like to thank Dr. Jane McKie and Dr. Jane Alexander, my PhD supervisors, who are immense sources of support. Dr. Alexander, in particular, has been my stalwart champion in reminding me that I am allowed to write the things I actually want to write, rather than submitting my work to an internalised Hayes Code. I am incredibly grateful.

Third, I want to thank my community of friends. Old friends from elementary school and high school and college, family friends from the

Smithsonian and old neighbourhoods and Photo Services, my parents' friends, my grandparents' friends, my teachers, my professors, my neighbours, my exes, my people from the Writers' Rooms, my therapist who I should probably not mention by name but who knows he would have a much longer item in this passage if I did — know that I see and am grateful for your support. It means the absolute world to me.

Thank you, specifically, to my writing community — but especially to Lindz McLeod and Claudia Menin. Lindz, I am so grateful for your guidance as I begin to navigate the professional writing world; I could not survive without your insight, your guidance, and your cats. I'm incredibly grateful for the opportunities you have thrown my way and can only hope to give back as much as I've received. Claudia, you know what I'm going to say here: I apologise for saying it in public, but here we go. I am so grateful to have you in my life. You're my best friend, my defender, and my writing partner. Thank you for loving my characters and their stories as much as I do. Thank you for knowing exactly what that means. (Also, thank you for being so annoying about the dishes, as you've just reminded me to say while I sit here writing.)

Finally, I would like to thank my family. My grandmothers, my aunts, my uncles — you have always been so wonderfully supportive of my career, and I do not know what I'd do without you. I'd like to acknowledge my grandfather, Roger, particularly: thank you for fostering my love of science fiction. All those volumes of Asimov's helped pave my way to here.

Mom, thank you for all the long editing sessions, the input on my work, and the pride you've always taken in my career. You've always been such a role model for me: you fight for the right thing against truly staggering odds, you consider the world carefully and thoughtfully, and you stand up so boldly to patriarchal norms. I'm incredibly proud to call you my mother.

Dad, thank you for all our conversations. Thank you for coming to so many of my conventions, signings, and readings. Thank you for the long talks about creative careers; for understanding what it means to have a creative career; and for being so proud of me, always, no matter what madness I'm up to. I cannot tell you how grateful I am. I'm so lucky to call you my father.

Post-finally, if you've made it this far: thank you, reader, for witnessing this story and the people who carry it. I know the ending may be tough, but they'll have other stories. Be assured, my darling, that ultimately it will be all right in the end.

ABOUT THE AUTHOR

Alex Penland is a former museum kid. They spent their childhood running rampant through the Smithsonian museums, which kicked off an early career as a child adventurer. Alex has worked in the field with NASA scientists, linguists, and acclaimed photographers.

Now twice a Pushcart-nominated author, Alex lives in Scotland while studying for a PhD in Creative Writing at the University of Edinburgh. Prior adventures include founding a writing organisation in Iowa, collaborating on micro-operas, diving with sharks, and volunteering with the Smithsonian for nearly a decade. Their work has been internationally published, appearing in *Interzone* and *Olney Magazine*. *Andrion* is their first novella.

Catch them on most social media channels as @AlexPenname, and find more information on their website: www.AlexPenland.com

THE CREDITS

Creating a book is a massive team effort.

Knight Errant and Alex Penland would like to thank everyone who worked behind the scenes to make *Andrion* happen.

Managing Director and Editor

Nathaniel Kunitsky

Publishing Assistant

Friday Schoemaker

Creative Director

Lenka Murová

Project Assistant

Angelica Curzi

Cover Art Illustrator

Jenni Coutts

A special thank you to every single person who backed and shared our Kickstarter campaign.

Without your support our 2023 list would not have been possible.

m. turner j. hudson gabriella b. page e. morrison julie l. penland l. kraus e. bowers
o. whitney h. duncan e. claybaugh friday lindz e. reed andreas p. casey y. mittal k. sietel
brigh w. mamuna k. allen k. vikings c. page l. o'brien c. wair a. stanback b. hughes r. novak
c. cox p. kimble m. otto elena noel e. r. craig d. skea i. g. morris e. pitner dpn marina
d. psmith c. barron j. bottles i. birman j. thompson k. blair s. mayer a. penland f. rossero
dlhalp s. lloyd o. pinchuk h. mcdaid m. paley c. lewis k. lennon C r. rush-morgan vince
j. l. smith w. hughes n. hardy a. mcquaid eris anna caith zaraegis s. dunlop b. cebulski
syksy r. jones g. gregory f. ostby Creative Scotland c. donaldson j. cooper h. hirst
r. mccleary c. alexandersson sara r. vance a. jehangir daniil b. norton ophelia j. alexander
l. burwitz d. malcom k. hunziker j. oui k. turner d. carol alexandra sian gareth s. jones
fitakaleerie j. q. peterson karen rós k. CM r. page claire a. frank a. traphagan missy cara
PG m. piper a. treacy d. penland n. briggs ninedin a. grunwald p. carroll jake a. vaughn
morgan holly f. daoinsidhe c. post p. sterk Argonaut Books e. thompson sam
g. felker-martin kimberly m.p. deutsch t. orosz connie c. brienne s. mcphail g. bard
s. ingram e. van doren rxbin ian r. heafield p. stanton s. mckinlay r. rusak r. tonks j. bay
sophie d. b. moose patience n. williams c. withers áine s. cole harriet j. cole s. pybus dokja
m. noone isabela k. guilliams j. tövissy MW anna a. anderson tenille adam shana i. m. leigh
l. croal el s. smalley bethany idontfindyouthatinteresting m. huxley p. strömberg t. wymore
t. bridges c. luca l. bradley l. burns n. queen r. lindstrom p. herterich a. r. cardno p. reitz
g. casillas s. kollman b. weiss k. macaskill-smith s. norman c. j. gibson k. frey simon c.
e. davidson rayanroar n. novak midnightmare s. fraser c. spann tania c. morton j. cleak
rachlette m. young l. kapusta j. osborne k. lovick scarlet g. mitchell l. benson j. curtis
rachel owlglass i. sheene

OTHER WORK BY KNIGHT ERRANT PRESS

F, M or Other: Quarrels with the Gender Binary

Queering the Map of Glasgow

Vicky Romeo Plus Joolz by Ely Percy

Love, Pan-Fried by Gray Crosbie

Tamlin by Aven Wildsmith

The False Sister by Briar Ripley Page

Andrion by Alex Penland

The Child of Hameln by Max Turner

ABOUT
KNIGHT ERRANT PRESS

Knight Errant Press is a queer micro press based in Falkirk, Scotland, established in 2017.

We have a focus on LGBTQIA+ and inter-sectional storytelling and creators, and work within most genres and print formats.

Showcasing new and emerging writers' careers is our ambition, and we strive to find 2 or 3 works a year to bring to the world.

You can find out more about us at www.knighterrantpress.com